**"Oh, look at him! He's beautiful. So majestic."
Rachel took her phone from her pocket and
took a few snaps of the deer at a safe distance.**

A second deer came to join the first, and then a third
and fourth, the color of their coats almost blending
with the bracken. The females grazed with the stag
looking over them, and Rachel stood watching them,
with Tim's arms wrapped round her and his cheek
pressed against hers.

"Aren't they stunning? This is the perfect Sunday
morning," he whispered against her ear. Then he kissed
the spot just behind her ear and sent desire licking up
her spine. She couldn't remember the last time she'd
felt that heady, powerful need to kiss someone, but she
acted on the impulse and turned around in his arms so
she could kiss him thoroughly.

When she broke the kiss, they were both shaking.

"I think a whole herd could've stomped past us just
now and we wouldn't have noticed," he said huskily.

She stole a last kiss. "You're telling me."

Dear Reader,

Christmas is a time of joy and light and warmth and hope. But it can also be a difficult time if you've lost someone over the holiday season. I still can't listen to "Please Come Home for Christmas," which was the first song on the radio after my mom died.

So we have Rachel, who loves Christmas, starting her new job as a consultant in the emergency department, and Tim, her boss, who finds Christmas difficult since losing his wife, who had loved Christmas so much.

Rachel, postdivorce, isn't looking for a relationship, but she wants to help her boss remember the good bits of Christmas. Except things don't quite go to plan, because in the process of saving Christmas for Tim, she manages to fall in love with him—and Tim falls in love with her.

Tim doesn't think it can work between them—he's let his late wife and his children down too often—but then an unexpected Christmas delivery changes everything…

I hope you enjoy Rachel and Tim's journey.

With love,

Kate Hardy

SAVING CHRISTMAS FOR THE ER DOC

―――

KATE HARDY

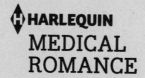

HARLEQUIN

MEDICAL
ROMANCE

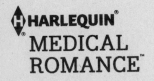

HARLEQUIN®
MEDICAL
ROMANCE™

Recycling programs
for this product may
not exist in your area.

ISBN-13: 978-1-335-73753-3

Saving Christmas for the ER Doc

Copyright © 2022 by Pamela Brooks

For questions and comments about the quality of this book, please contact us at CustomerService@Harlequin.com.

Harlequin Enterprises ULC
22 Adelaide St. West, 41st Floor
Toronto, Ontario M5H 4E3, Canada
www.Harlequin.com

Printed in U.S.A.

Kate Hardy has always loved books, and could read before she went to school. She discovered Harlequin books when she was twelve, and decided that this was what she wanted to do. When she isn't writing Kate enjoys reading, cinema, ballroom dancing and the gym. You can contact her via her website: katehardy.com.

Books by Kate Hardy

Harlequin Medical Romance

Twin Docs' Perfect Match

Second Chance with Her Guarded GP
Baby Miracle for the ER Doc

Changing Shifts

Fling with Her Hot-Shot Consultant

Their Pregnancy Gift
Carrying the Single Dad's Baby
Heart Surgeon, Prince…Husband!
A Nurse and a Pup to Heal Him
Mistletoe Proposal on the Children's Ward
Forever Family for the Midwife
Surgeon's Second Chance in Florence

Visit the Author Profile page at Harlequin.com for more titles.

To Chris and Chloe, who brought back
the wonder of Christmas for me.

CHAPTER ONE

NEW JOB, NEW HOSPITAL, and Rachel Halliday was really looking forward to her new start. She'd switched back to her maiden name, and nobody in her new department needed to know how miserable the last couple of years had been. They'd just see Rachel for herself: a good doctor, a supportive colleague, and hopefully a new friend.

Rachel's best friend, Jenny, was a cardiac surgeon at Muswell Hill Memorial Hospital's sister hospital; she'd seen the job on the trust's bulletin board and urged Rachel to apply for it. Rachel had refused; her eldest daughter Meg was in her Finals year at university in Manchester and Saskia, her youngest, was just starting university in Sheffield, so how could she add yet more disruption to the girls' lives? Even though the job was a sideways move and would fit perfectly—a consultant in the Emergency Department, with some responsibility for teaching—she'd resigned herself to sticking it out at Hampstead for another year. By then, she hoped that the pity among her colleagues would surely have died down and something else would've taken her place as the topic to be gossiped about. And if it hadn't—well, then she'd go for the new start.

But Jenny had enlisted Meg and Saskia's support, and Rachel's daughters had set up a family video call to nag her into applying for the job.

'Mum, you've had a horrible two years, with Gran having dementia and you supporting her before she died, and Dad doing what he did, and then the divorce. It's time you did something for *you*,' Saskia said.

'And I've checked out the commute. It's half an hour on the Tube and then a walk through the park, so you don't even have to move house—though, if you decide that's what you want to do, we'll back you,' Meg added. 'We'll even come home and scrub grouting and tidy everything out of sight, ready for the estate agency to take photos.'

'Thank you, both of you, but I'm not planning to move house right now,' Rachel said. Moving house was meant to be one of the three most stressful life events, along with bereavement and divorce; after going through two of them in the last year, she needed a break before she could even consider the third.

'But you can still apply for the job,' Saskia encouraged her.

'They'll be lucky to have you, Mum,' Meg agreed. 'I know it's a sideways move, but it'll be a fresh start—and a new place means new opportunities. Go for it.'

So Rachel had given in to her daughters' urging and applied. She'd been invited for an interview; a few days later, to her delight, she'd been offered the job. And now today, on a foggy and freezing morning in mid-October, she was walking through the park from the Tube station to the hospital, enjoying the way the trees loomed like shadowy blobs and became more like intricate sculptures as she drew closer to them. She loved this time of year, even though today the ground was slippery underfoot and no doubt the waiting room this morning would be full of patients with Colles' fractures who'd put their arms out to stop themselves hitting the ground face-first and broken their wrists. She'd nearly fallen over, herself, just outside the Tube station.

Today was her induction day, but hopefully they could rattle through all the admin stuff fairly quickly and she could get straight into doing what she loved most: treating patients and teaching her juniors. She was looking forward to getting to know her new colleagues. She'd liked what she'd seen of Tim Hughes, the head of the department, at her interview; he'd seemed both friendly and super-calm—just what was needed in the rush of the Emergency Department.

But the second she went to the reception desk to introduce herself and explain that she was due to start in the department today but hadn't been given her key card yet, the receptionist put a hand on her arm and shook her head. 'I'm sorry, Miss Halliday. Mr Hughes sends his apologies, but your induction's going to have to be moved. He's asked if I can direct you straight to Resus, instead. There's been a bit of a bad pile-up on the M1 and they're expecting several patients.'

Given the weather conditions, Rachel wasn't surprised to hear there had been at least one car accident. With a busy motorway and several vehicles involved, it sounded as if the department was going to be stretched. 'Not a problem. Can you tell me where to go, please?'

'I've got the key to your locker.' The receptionist handed over a key with the locker number on the fob. 'The changing room's first on the left through the corridor—there are scrubs on the shelf—and the staff room's next door. Resus is at the end of the corridor, and one of the team there will tell you which room they need you in. It'll be on the whiteboard, too.'

'Great. Thank you very much.'

It didn't take Rachel long to change into green scrubs and her work shoes and dump everything else in her locker, and then she hurried down the corridor to Resus, where she recognised the man standing in front of the whiteboard—Tim Hughes, the head of the department, who'd interviewed her for the job. He was tall, with short dark hair greying at the temples, and the most amazing cornflower-blue eyes that had made her pulse leap inappropriately at the interview.

And now was an even more inappropriate time to remember that flare of attraction. The department was about to become super-busy and there was no room for day-dreaming.

'Hi, I'm Rachel Halliday. I believe you're expecting me?' she asked.

Tim nodded. 'Yes—welcome to the team. Sorry your induction day's been hijacked.'

'It's fine, Mr Hughes.'

'Tim,' he corrected. 'We don't stand on ceremony here.'

'Rachel,' she said. 'Reception told me there's been a situation on the M1.'

'Yes. We think one of the drivers had a heart attack, veered across the road and hit the central reservation. The car behind him braked to try and avoid him, but several other cars didn't manage to stop in time.'

Hence the pile-up, Rachel thought. 'What do we know about our patients?'

'There's the one with a suspected heart attack; Sam Price, one of the other consultants, is treating him. I'm dealing with the critical patient with head injuries; there are a few with suspected fractures, and others with soft tissue injuries and shock. We're expecting the ambulances in any minute now, and I'm putting you in Resus Three with Ediye Mosaku to treat a driver who hit the steering wheel. The ambulance crew think he might have a flail chest,' Tim said, gesturing to the whiteboard on the wall. 'The other patients will be triaged as they get here.'

'Got it,' she said.

'This is Ediye,' he said as a young doctor in scrubs walked into the corridor. 'Ediye, this is Rachel.'

'Our new consultant. Lovely to meet you,' Ediye said with a broad smile.

'Perhaps we can catch up later today, Rachel, when things have quietened down,' Tim said.

'Sure,' she said cheerfully. Though, in her experience, things never really quietened down in the Emergency Department.

He smiled back. 'Good. The coffees will be on me.' There was a yell of, 'Tim!' from Resus One. 'Sounds as if my patient's arrived. See you later.'

Funny how that smile made her heart feel as if it had done a backflip.

Rachel made herself damp down the renewed flare of attraction. She needed to get a grip. Tim Hughes looked as if he was only a couple of years older than she was, and the odds were that he was already in a long-established relationship. If he was single, then he'd probably have as much emotional baggage as she had. Besides, even if he was single and the attraction turned out to be mutual, she wasn't looking for a relationship—not after the events of the past year. Right at the moment, Rachel's focus was on finding out who she was, now she was fifty-two and divorced, and working out what she wanted from life. Starting all over again, trying to find a new partner, just felt like a step too far. She wasn't ready to trust her heart to anyone.

Hoping none of that had shown on her face—she'd be mortified if her new colleagues had spotted that little leap of attraction, or the way she'd talked herself out of it—she turned to Ediye. 'Because it's my first day, obviously I don't know who everyone is yet or what their roles are. But I don't want to patronise anyone by behaving as if they don't know a thing when they're really experienced or push them too far out of their comfort zone by expecting them to know more than they actually do.' She smiled. 'So can I start with you, please?'

Ediye laughed. 'Sure. I've just finished my F2 year, and I'm in my first year of the

Acute Care Common Stem training programme. Emergency was my favourite rotation, so I jumped at the chance to join the team. Tim's a really good head of department—he drills it into everyone that you ask if you're not sure about something, and he tries to give the junior doctors as much experience as possible.'

'Brilliant,' Rachel said. It was the impression she'd had at her interview, too, and the way she liked working. 'Have you dealt with a flail chest before?'

'I've seen a couple, and I know the theory,' Ediye said.

'In that case, I'm happy to let you lead, and I'll only step in if I think you need a hand. Ask me whatever you need to know as we're treating our patient; if you need me to take over, that's absolutely fine, and then afterwards we'll have a debrief so we can go over any decisions I made and I'll explain why I chose that particular option.' She smiled. 'Or, rather, you can tell me why I made those decisions, and I'll steer you in the right direction if I need to.'

'That'd be really good,' Ediye said.

A few seconds later, the first three batches

of paramedics rushed in. Rachel and Ediye had the last patient, Ben Anstey; once the handover had been done, Rachel introduced them.

'Hello, Ben—I'm Rachel and this is Ediye. We're Emergency Department doctors in Muswell Hill Memorial Hospital, and we'll be looking after you today. The paramedics tell us you hit the steering wheel, and we think you might have broken some ribs.'

'I think so, too, because they hurt like hell,' Ben said, his face pinched.

'We'll give you some pain relief, but first can you take a deep breath for me?'

He did so and winced.

Rachel nodded at Ediye, encouraging the younger doctor to take over.

'It hurts when you take a deep breath?' Ediye asked.

'And when I move,' Ben confirmed. 'It's hard to breathe.' He coughed, and winced. 'Ow. That hurts my shoulder as well.'

'OK. I'm going to put you on an oxygen mask now,' Ediye said. 'That'll help you breathe more easily. I want to examine you, take your temperature and listen to your chest, if that's all right?'

'Whatever you need to do to stop it hurting,' Ben said.

Ediye put him on oxygen and gave him pain relief, then checked his stats and turned to Rachel. 'His temperature's up, his heart rate's too high, his blood pressure's falling and he's got falling oxygen sats,' she said a low voice. 'I notice that part of his chest goes in when he breathes in and out when he breathes out, so I think the paramedics were right about it being flail chest.' Flail chest was a condition where at least three ribs in a row had two or more breaks, so part of the chest wall separated from the rest and moved independently. 'There are decreased breath sounds, so I want to send him for a CT scan to check out trauma to the lungs.'

'Good call,' Rachel said. 'And a possible pneumothorax, because he's got that dry cough and the pain when he breathes radiates to his shoulder.' A pneumothorax was where air leaked into the space between the lung and the chest wall; the pressure of the trapped air then caused the lung to collapse.

Ediye explained to Ben what would happen next and checked if he wanted them to call anyone.

Once the results were back, Rachel reviewed them with the younger doctor. 'Flail chest, a pneumothorax, and the beginnings of contusions to the lungs—all quite common in cases of blunt trauma where you're slammed against the steering wheel,' Rachel said. 'What's your treatment plan?'

'We'll call the thoracic SPR to review the scan and see if they want to take him to Theatre to stabilise his ribs,' Ediye said. 'Meanwhile we need to get the air out from the pleural space, so his lung can reinflate and to reduce his pain.'

'Perfect; but, given that he has flail chest as well, I'd go straight to a chest drain in this case,' Rachel said. 'Have you done one before?'

'I've seen a couple and done one,' Ediye said.

It seemed that Tim Hughes definitely acted on what he'd said at the interview, Rachel thought, pleased. 'Good. You can do this one and talk me through it as if you're teaching me. We need to make sure Ben has enough pain relief so he can take deep breaths, cough and move around—that'll help him to avoid a chest infection. I'll call his wife while you call Thoracics.'

When Ben came back from his CT scan,

Rachel said, 'Your wife's on her way in. Reception will send her straight in to us when she gets here.'

'Thank you,' Ben said.

Ediye explained the results of his scan and what they were going to do next. Once Ediye had done the chest drain under Rachel's supervision, Rachel took Ben through some breathing exercises for him to do on the ward to help keep his chest clear.

Ben's wife arrived; Ediye introduced them, explained what they'd done and what was happening next, and finished with, 'If you'd like to sit with him, the thoracic specialist will be with you soon. If you're worried about anything in the meantime, talk to one of the nurses and they can call us in if necessary.'

When they'd left Ben but before seeing their next patient, Rachel smiled at Ediye. 'You did really well with that drain.'

Ediye looked pleased. 'Thanks. Telling you what I was going to do really helped me focus.'

'Good. Let's go and find our next patient.'

It was an incredibly busy morning; as well as the patients from the motorway crash, the waiting room was full of people who'd slipped on the ice and sprained an ankle or fractured a wrist or hurt a knee. Monday morning was always the busiest time in the Emergency Department, and it was way past lunchtime before Rachel had the chance to make herself a coffee in the staff kitchen. She added some cold water so she could drink it down straight away.

'You must be Rachel,' one of the nurses said when she walked in. 'I was just coming to find you. Tim's in his office and asked if you'd come and see him when you've got a moment.'

So much for her break, Rachel thought, and drained her coffee. 'OK. Can I ask where his office is?'

'In the corridor opposite here, at the end on the right,' the nurse said with a smile.

'Thank you.' Rachel washed up her mug and left it on the draining board, then headed for Tim's office.

At the rap on his door, Tim called, 'Come in!'

As he'd hoped, rather than it being one of the suits with yet more paperwork to dump on his desk, their new consultant walked in. 'I believe you wanted to see me?' Rachel asked.

'Yes.' His eyes narrowed. 'It's been crazy this morning. Have you had a break, yet?'

'I was planning to have one now. I just grabbed a coffee in the staff room,' she said, 'and I was about to get the emergency chocolate bar from my bag.'

It was par for the course when they were as busy as they'd been that morning, but Tim didn't like the extra pressure on his staff. 'We can do better than that,' he said. 'I'll take you to the canteen and buy you a sandwich.' He could see the beginning of protest on her face and added, 'No strings. It's your first day and, with that crash, you were pretty much chucked in at the deep end. Plus, we can multi-task. Debrief and lunch at the same time.'

'All right. Thank you. To be honest, I'm glad the induction's been shoved out of the way,' she admitted as she followed him out of his office, and they walked down the corridor together. 'I'd rather be helping patients than spending hours going through admin stuff that I could sort out at home.'

A woman after his own heart. He liked

that. 'How's your man with flail chest?' he asked.

'We've admitted him, and the thoracic team are going to let me know what they're doing. Ediye did the chest drain for the pneumothorax. She said she'd done one, so I went by the "see one, do one, teach one" principle and got her to talk me through it as she did it. And she was great.'

Tim approved of Rachel's no-nonsense attitude; he'd liked her at the interview and thought she'd fit in well to the team. It was good to know his instincts had been spot on. They'd never let him down in his job. It was a pity they'd let him down in his personal life. If he'd paid more attention at home, if he'd let someone else take over here and gone out to dinner that night with Mandy and their friends instead of working late because he'd wanted to make sure his patient made it, maybe she wouldn't have—

He shoved the thought aside. *Not now.*

At the canteen, he bought them both coffee, sandwiches and cake.

'How was your guy with the head injury?' she asked.

'We got him as far as Intensive Care,' he said, 'and now it's a waiting game. The guy with the heart attack didn't quite make it here, and Sam had been called to treat someone else, so I had to talk to the poor guy's husband and tell him what had happened—which is why I'm eating my cake before my sandwich.' He grimaced. 'I hate breaking the news that makes someone's world crumble.' He'd been on the receiving end of news like that, two years ago, and it had taken him quite a while to get back to coping. His girls still called him every day to check on him; and every day he put his work face on and told them he was doing fine. Which he was—at work. It was home that was tough, especially walking in through the front door to be greeted with silence instead of hearing Mandy bustling about or humming along with the radio as she marked an essay. He didn't even have a dog to welcome him home; much as he would've liked the company, it simply wouldn't be fair on the poor animal, not with the hours he worked.

Maybe he needed a fish.

But a fish couldn't cuddle into you...

Stop. Stop it now. Remember what the counsellor said: focus on the positives. Think of everything you have to be thankful about, everything from the big things to the little ones. The girls, your job, your grand-child-to-be. Your health. Good coffee and loud music.

'Anyway, welcome to Muswell Hill Memorial Hospital.' He lifted his forkful of cake in a toast.

'Thank you.' His eyes caught hers and he realised just how pretty Rachel Halliday was, with those huge grey eyes. Her salt-and-pepper brown hair was cut into a neat bob that framed her heart-shaped face perfectly, and her mouth was a perfect cupid's bow.

Oh, for pity's sake. He knew from her application form that his new consultant was a couple of years younger than he was, and he'd guess her life stage was very similar to his own; she probably had grown-up children who were finding their own way in the world, and maybe the first grandchild was about to make an appearance. Thinking about how pretty she was really wasn't appropriate.

She's here to talk about work, he reminded himself.

'It's not usually *quite* this mad here on a Monday morning.'

'With all that ice, I was expecting a slew

of Colles' fractures,' she said. 'I nearly fell
flat on my face when I came out of the Tube
station.' She smiled. 'Just as well I managed
to stay upright, because it would've been a
bit embarrassing if I'd turned up in the waiting room on my first day, needing a back
slab on my wrist instead of prescribing one
for someone else.'

'Just a tad,' he said, smiling back. 'I'm
guessing you already know where the lock-
ers and changing rooms are, and the staff
kitchen.'

'And now you've shown me where the
café is, so I'm pretty much sorted. I just need
my key card so I don't have to keep asking
Reception to let me in, and my login details so I can access patient records and my
email—we did all the notes under Ediye's
log-in today.' She looked hopeful. 'Can we
skip the rest of it?'

'What, you mean the health and safety
bits, the fire procedures, the online policy,
the...' He chuckled at the rising dismay in
her expression. 'I'll have a word with HR
and see if they can give us a workaround.
Or maybe one of them will agree to do it as
a one-to-one or something and cut it down
to half an hour. I'm pretty sure there isn't

that much difference between how we do things here and how they did things at your last hospital.'

'Thank you,' she said. 'I don't mind reading stuff or doing an online induction course in my own time, if that helps.'

'Won't your family mind?' The question came out before he could stop it. 'Sorry. Forget I asked that. It was intrusive.'

'No, it's fine. My daughters are both at uni, so they're only home during the holidays.'

So his guess had been right. She was at a similar life stage to him, with grown-up children, though hers were clearly a few years younger than his. But he noticed that she hadn't mentioned a husband or partner. Mandy had always been a bit fed up with how much time his job took up, and they'd argued about it a lot. Was it the same for other senior doctors? Did her partner get fed up with her always being late home?

Tim couldn't help glancing at Rachel's left hand and noticed that it was bare. There was a bare-below-the-elbow hygiene policy for clinical staff, but plain rings were allowed. Maybe her wedding ring wasn't plain, then. Or maybe she and her partner hadn't bothered getting married. Not that it was any of his business.

But then she said, 'Actually, the girls pushed me into applying for the job here. I'm glad they did.'

'Pushed you?' He was surprised.

She nodded. 'I was going to stick it out in Hampstead for another year, because it's Meg's final year at uni and Saskia's first year, and I think they've had enough disruption over the last few months without me changing everything on top of that.'

Disruption? It sounded as if life had been tricky for her, and he needed to back off rather than risk making things awkward for her. 'Kids are often more resilient than we give them credit for,' he said. His girls had coped with losing their mother a lot better than he had. Possibly because they'd been able to cry, and he'd stuffed his feelings down. The only times he'd cried in public was when his daughters had been born, and he'd brushed away a tear at their weddings. At Mandy's funeral he'd kept himself under rigid control, knowing that if he let himself crack he'd never piece himself back together.

And he knew, too, that he'd kept his girls at more of an emotional distance than he really wanted to, because he didn't want to lean on them and be a burden. Sometimes he wondered if he'd taken it too far; was he disconnected from them instead of protecting them? And, if so, how was he going to reconnect with them? Mandy would've known how to handle things—but Mandy wasn't here any more.

'My eldest is going on maternity leave in about three weeks,' he said.

'Will it be your first grandchild?' Rachel asked. At his nod, she said, 'You and your partner must really be looking forward to it.'

'Just me, actually,' he said quietly. 'My wife died two years ago.' He blew out a breath. 'Actually, you might as well hear it from me, because someone in the department's bound to tell you, but the rule is no pity, OK?'

'OK.'

Her grey eyes were sympathetic rather than pitying, and that gave him the courage to tell her. 'Mandy had a severe sesame allergy,' he said. 'She was out having dinner with friends—I was supposed to be joining them, but I was held up here.' Even though he knew that her death wasn't his fault, that he couldn't have saved her, that nothing would've changed even if he'd been there, he still felt guilty. If he'd been at dinner with her like he'd promised, at least he could've held her hand in the ambulance and told her he loved her.

But he hadn't been there. He'd been at work.

'Obviously they'd double-checked it with the staff, but there was a mix-up in the kitchen. Nobody realised at the time, but the food had been accidentally cooked in sesame oil. She collapsed, and then she hit her head in the wrong place.' And then there was the bit that had hacked the bottom out of his world. 'She died in the ambulance on the way to hospital.'

'I'm sorry. That's tough, losing your wife so young—and not getting the chance to say goodbye,' Rachel said, reaching across the table to squeeze his hand briefly.

He appreciated the small gesture of kindness. 'Yeah. It's the things you didn't get time to share that you miss the most,' he said. Their first grandchild, due in a few weeks. Their youngest daughter's wedding, last year. Growing old together. All their plans. All the things they hadn't shared because he'd been busy at work; and how ironic it was that now he worked even harder, to fill the gaps and make himself too tired to think when he got home.

'It's not quite the same thing,' she said, 'but I get where you're coming from because I lost my mum earlier this year.' She looked sad. 'In a way, I lost her before she died, because she had dementia. I took a sabbatical to care for her as long as I could.'

'Dementia's a cruel disease,' he said. 'The way it takes someone bit by bit.'

She nodded. 'It was hard on the girls. Towards the end, their gran kept mistaking them for me when I was their age. But Saskia would sit and read to Mum every evening before dinner, and when Meg was home from uni she'd play the guitar and get Mum to sing old Beatles songs with her.' She smiled. 'She used to do a video call from uni every Wednesday night and get her grandmother singing along with us all.'

'Apparently, music's one of the last memories to go,' Tim said. 'So your mum lived with you?'

'For six months or so. She wasn't safe to live on her own, even with carers popping in,' Rachel said. 'That's why I took time off work and she moved in with us—until she got to the stage where she needed more care than I could give her on my own. Then, much as I hated the idea, I had to find a nursing home.'

He remembered now that the gap in Rachel's CV had come up in her interview, and she'd quietly said she'd taken a break from work to help a family member. Now he understood.

'But I'm glad I spent that time with her. And I guess it did me a favour because it gave my husband the final excuse to leave me for girlfriend number...' She shrugged. 'Well, whatever number she was.'

Her husband had dumped her during her mother's final illness? He winced. 'That's tough.' Not just the affair, but the timing. Even though Mandy's mum was really difficult, Tim wouldn't have complained if she'd had a terminal illness and Mandy had wanted to move her into their home to look after her in her final months. When you were partners, you took the rough with the smooth and you supported each other; you didn't just go off and find someone else with fewer complications when things got difficult. Rachel's ex clearly hadn't shared Tim's views.

'It's been a bit of a tricky couple of years,' Rachel said.

And that was a huge understatement, Tim thought.

'But the girls and I got through it.' She smiled. 'And now I get to do something for me: a new start in a new job. No pity or set-up dates required.'

'Oh, the set-up dates.' He groaned. 'Tell me about it. I know people mean well. But when friends invite you to dinner, and you think you're simply going to spend a nice evening with friends you've known and loved for years, eating and talking too much; and then you turn up and they introduce you to someone suitable, and there's all the expectation…' He shook his head. 'Not my idea of fun.'

'At our age, if that "someone suitable" has always been single, I've found they tend to be very set in their ways,' she said. 'And I've had enough of having to bend over back-wards to please someone else.'

It sounded as if her ex had been a bit de-manding, Tim thought. 'Absolutely. And, if they're divorced or widowed, there's a bro-ken heart to deal with on top of your own. Dating isn't for me. I'm perfectly happy to be on my own.' It wasn't quite true—he was horribly lonely, and the house echoed—but at the same time he wasn't quite ready to join the dating mill. Especially at this time of year. He was dreading the run-up to Christmas. All the songs of loneliness that seemed to be on every radio station, whatever one he flicked to; all the reminders of happy families, when his own was fractured.

'I'm happy on my own, too,' she said, raising her own coffee.

'And that's why I've learned to eat cake before sandwiches,' he said. 'Do the happy stuff first.'

'That's a great idea. Except,' she said, gesturing to her own plate, 'when the sandwich happens to be a hot brie and cranberry panini. Then I'm afraid there's no contest. Cheese first, all the way.'

'You're a cheese fiend?' he asked.

'Totally,' she admitted.

'Then there's a shop I need to introduce you to,' he said. 'Which I guarantee will make me your new best friend.'

She laughed. 'I like the sound of that, though you'll have to make do with being second-best friend, or else Jenny—my bestie—will scalp you. Let's just say she's a cardiac surgeon who does kickboxing in her spare time.'

'Super-scary, so don't mess with her. Got it. Second-best friend will do fine,' he said, and lifted his mug. 'Here's to new friends.'

'New friends,' she echoed.

How weird that her smile made him feel more settled than he'd been in months. Not that he was going to examine that too closely. 'Right. What else do you need to know about the department? We have team nights out, every so often—anything from cocktails to curry to clubbing.' He smiled at her. 'And other things that begin with a different letter of the alphabet.'

'Pints, pizza and...let me see...paddle-boarding at Paddington Basin?' she suggested.

He couldn't help laughing. 'Nice one.' Instinctively, he liked this woman. Rachel was definitely on his wavelength and she seemed to share his sense of humour, too. 'I admit, I tend to skip the clubbing nights. Not because I'm too old, but because the music's not quite my scene.' He grinned. 'I still tease my girls, though. I threaten to take them clubbing, wear a really loud and embarrassing shirt, get the DJ to play something especially for me, and have a good old dad dance right in the middle of the dance floor—making sure everyone knows I'm with them.'

She looked sad for a moment. 'Steve wouldn't even consider saying that as a joke, let alone really go somewhere with them. He doesn't bother doing anything with the girls.' She shook herself. 'Sorry. Ignore me. Not your problem.'

Or his business, he thought. 'Would you go clubbing with your girls?'

'Probably not—like you, the music isn't my scene—but I still go to the odd gig with them. They love Bryan Adams as much as I do, so I take them with me to see him whenever he plays in London,' she said. 'There's really nothing better than singing your head off to songs you love with thousands of other people.'

'Loud enough so the band has to turn the sound up. I agree. That's the best sort of stadium gig,' he said. 'Though I have to admit I love the tiny venues as well, when there's maybe fifty of you and a seriously good guitarist.'

'I'm hoping to find something they'll both like when they're home for the Christmas holidays.' She smiled. 'I love Christmas.'

Whereas Tim found it incredibly hard to bear, nowadays. But he was the head of the department, and his staff had to come before his feelings. 'Now you've mentioned Christmas, make sure you catch up with Ediye before you go today. She's in charge of organising the department Christmas meal and Secret Santa this year, so she'll get your name on the list. It's the last week of November.'

'I'll do that,' she said. 'And I'd better get back to work. We still have a waiting room full of patients.'

'Not to mention the joys of paperwork. And I have a meeting with the suits this afternoon, so I need to play nice.' He rolled his eyes.

'Thank you for lunch,' she said, 'and for making me feel welcome.'

'Pleasure.'

And how strange it was, Tim thought as they chatted on the way back to the department, that he felt lighter of heart than he had for a long, long time. Something about Rachel Halliday made him feel as if the world was in kilter again. Or maybe it was just the relief of knowing that they'd made the right choice in appointing her: a warm, lovely woman who would be great with the patients and staff alike. Of course it was that. Work. It had to be.

CHAPTER TWO

'I'M SORRY I couldn't make dinner last night,' Jenny said.

'You're a surgeon, Jen. You can hardly stop in the middle of an operation and tell the rest of your team that you have dinner plans and they'll just have to carry on without you,' Rachel said. 'It was fine. I got your message, and I had stuff in the fridge so I could make myself dinner.'

'Which had better not mean just a cheese sandwich,' Jenny said.

'A toasted cheese sandwich—with good bread, chutney and a salad—is one of life's joys,' Rachel said. 'No, actually. For your information, it was salmon baked with lemon and thyme, roasted veggies and wilted greens.'

'Mediterranean food. Just what a cardiac

surgeon likes to hear,' Jenny said. 'So how was your first day in your new job?'

'Great. The team's lovely, and Tim, the head of the department, is one of the good guys—he managed to talk HR into letting me do most of the induction stuff online. *And* he bought me a brie and cranberry panini to welcome me to the team.' She grinned. 'So I got my cheese fix yesterday anyway.'

'Sounds good. And how are the girls?'

'Saskia's settled in really well, Meg's busy planning her dissertation, and they're doing tag team texts to nag me to eat properly. Which,' Rachel said, 'is probably in collusion with their godmother.'

Jenny batted her eyelashes. 'I couldn't possibly comment.'

Rachel laughed and raised her glass of red wine in a toast. 'Thank you. It's good to know you all have my back.'

'Of course we do.' Jenny smiled. 'We love you.'

'I love you, too. And I'm so glad you're not doing the set-up dates any more. Tim said it's the same for him.'

'He's divorced?'

'Widowed. Don't get ideas,' Rachel said, seeing the interest on her best friend's face and guessing what Jenny was thinking. 'We're going to be friends.'

'It's always good to make new friends,' Jenny said. 'But I still worry about you being lonely.'

'I have my girls, I have you, I have other friends and I love my job. All the loose ends are tied up with Steve. Apart from wishing I'd had the sense to ask him to leave, years ago, I'm doing fine,' Rachel said with a smile. Tim Hughes really was going to be just friends with her. He understood that she wasn't ready to start all over again, because he was in exactly the same place that she was. Friends was good. Friends would be enough.

And she wasn't going to think about the way his cornflower-blue eyes crinkled at the corners and made her heart do a little skip.

'Hello, love.' Tim handed his daughter a bouquet of bright orange gerberas. Flowers weren't really enough to bridge the gap he suspected he'd put between them, but it was a start. And you didn't always have to say things out loud, did you?

'Oh, Dad. They're gorgeous. Thank you.' Hannah gave him a hug. 'Oof. Either you've got fatter since last week or I have,' she teased, 'because I can't get my arms all the way round you.'

Tim chuckled and rested his hand on the bump. 'Good evening, little one.' His smile broadened when the baby kicked in response. 'Knows their granddad's voice, I see.'

'Good, because we're so lining you up for babysitting duties. Come and sit down while I put these in water.'

'You're the one who should be sitting down, not me.' He took the flowers back. 'Sit. Just remind me where you keep your vases and tell me which one you want.'

'Were you this bossy when Mum was pregnant with me?' Hannah asked.

'Absolutely. So there's no standing at the top of a stepladder to paint the nursery ceiling. If you want it done, ask Jamal or me. Got it?' His heart ached. This was when Hannah needed her mum to tell her all the little stories about what it had been like to be pregnant with her, to share the experiences and reassure her and make her laugh instead of worrying. But Mandy wasn't here—and Tim could only tell Hannah stuff from the outside, not how it actually felt to carry a baby. 'Your mum rested when I told her to, though she refused to put up with my cooking. You're lucky that Jamal can cook, because if you'd had to rely on me you would've been stuck with scorched baked beans on burnt toast every day of the week for months.'

She looked at him. 'Dad, you are—?'

'Yes, of course I'm eating properly,' he cut in, reassuring her. 'I'm not that bad. Half of what I tell you about my cooking is for dramatic purposes.'

'Not convincing, Dad—I used to live with you, remember.' But she let him usher her into the kitchen, directed him to the cupboard where she kept her vases, and sat down at the table while he put the flowers in water and started making them both a mug of tea.

'So how's your week been?' she asked.

'Good. My new consultant started on Monday. Just as I'd hoped, she fits in very well with the team.'

'Consultant?' Hannah looked interested. 'So she must be in at least her late thirties, then.'

'She's nearer my age, actually,' he said.

'Oh.' Hannah raised an eyebrow. 'Would she be single?'

He rolled his eyes. 'Don't *you* start. Actually, she is, but don't get any ideas. I think we'll become friends, but no more than that.' Even if Rachel Halliday was really pretty and had a warmth that drew him, he wasn't looking for love. He was just getting through the days. 'Nobody will ever match up to your mum, Han.'

'Soph and I don't want you to be lonely, Dad,' Hannah said. 'Mum wouldn't have wanted that, either. And it's been two and a half years. That's a long time to be on your own.'

'I know, love.' He brought their mugs of tea over. 'And I'm fine as I am. Really.' It wasn't strictly true, but Tim didn't want his daughter worrying about him. He'd find his way through this, in his own time. 'Now, tell me about your week.'

On Thursday morning, the paramedics rushed in with a middle-aged man who'd been cutting wood with an electric saw. They'd called the department beforehand, so Rachel had already got the surgeon and anaesthetist on standby, and when the patient arrived she asked Lorraine, the triage nurse, to bleep the surgeon.

'I'm Rachel, one of the doctors, and I'll be looking after you today,' she said.

'Dave Fleetwood,' he said, 'but everyone calls me Woody because of my name and because of what I do.'

'OK, Woody. Can you tell me what happened?' Rachel asked.

'I was cutting some wood. It slipped, and my left hand ended up under the blade,' he said. 'I'm not sure how bad it is because I blacked out and Baz—my best mate, and thank God he was working with me—put my fingers in a plastic bag with ice.'

'That's quick thinking.' The situation was time-critical, Rachel knew. The longer that the blood supply had been cut to a body part, the lower the chances were that the surgeons could reattach it. From the amount of blood on the dressing covering his hand, it looked as if this case could be tricky.

'I'll give you some pain relief,' she said, 'and the surgeon's on his way down. I'm going to send you—and the fingers your friend saved—for an X-ray, so we can get a better idea of whether we're looking at crush injuries as well as laceration and what the surgeon's going to need to do. Can you remember when you last had a tetanus vaccination booster?'

He shook his head. 'No idea.'

'We'll add that in,' she said. 'Did you hit your head at all when you blacked out?'

'No,' he said. 'Baz caught me and sat me on a chair.'

'That's good. Can I ask, how old was the blade?'

'Pretty new,' he said, 'so hopefully it doesn't mean there was any gunk on the blade and it's not going to get infected.'

She unwrapped the dressing; there were three fingers missing, and his little finger looked damaged as well. 'OK. I'll clean this up, give you some pain relief and a tetanus jab, and then we'll get you to X-Ray. Can we call anyone for you?'

'Baz called my missus when the ambulance came,' he said. 'She's on her way in now. I feel so bad about this. We were supposed to be going away, this weekend. It's our wedding anniversary. But I'm not going to be able to drive us there, and she can't drive.' He bit his lip. 'We'll book a taxi. I'll be out of hospital by then, won't I?'

'That's one to ask the surgeon,' she said with a sympathetic smile.

The surgeon had come down to the department by the time the X-ray files were through to her computer.

'This isn't looking great,' Mr Gupta said as they reviewed the X-rays together. 'You can see there's a lot of damage to his little finger as well as the three he's severed. I'll try to save as many of his fingers as I can, but with that level of damage I think he's going to need to prepare for the worst.'

'Poor guy,' Rachel said.

Lorraine came into the office. 'Rachel, I've got Mrs Fleetwood in the relatives' room. The whiteboard says her husband's with you.'

'Yes. He's on his way back from X-Ray,' Rachel said. 'We'll come with you to collect her.'

In the relatives' room, Lorraine introduced the anxious-looking woman as Suze Fleetwood.

'Is Woody going to be all right? I mean, Baz said on the phone he'd cut half his fingers off. He lives for his job. If he can't do stuff with wood any more, I just don't know what he'll…' Looking distressed, Suze shook her head.

'Mrs Fleetwood, let me introduce you to Mr Gupta, the hand surgeon,' Rachel said gently. 'He'll be helping your husband in Theatre.'

'I'm going to do my very best for your husband, Mrs Fleetwood, and I'm good at my job, but I'm afraid I need you to prepare yourself for the fact I might not be able to save all his fingers,' Mr Gupta said. 'It's going to be a very long operation. I'd say it's likely to take more than twelve hours, so I'd advise you to either get some rest at home or call some family or friends to come and be with you, because waiting here on your own will give you too much time to worry.'

'Twelve *hours*?' Suze looked shocked. 'And you might not…' She dragged in a breath. 'Working with wood—that's what he loves, more than anything. Making furniture. He's a proper craftsman. If he can't do that any more, then it'll be the end of the world for him.' She looked distraught.

'We'll do our best for him,' Mr Gupta said gently. 'And we can do a lot with prosthetics, nowadays. Rehab will take time, but with support I promise we'll be able to help him. He doesn't have to lose everything.'

'Can I see him before he has the operation?'

'Of course you can,' Rachel said. 'He's on his way back from X-Ray now.'

'You can come to the doors of the operating theatre with him,' Mr Gupta added, 'but then, as I said earlier, I'd advise getting someone to come and sit with you in the cafeteria or the relatives' room. We'll let you know as soon as there's any news.'

'Let's go and wait for him at the cubicle,' Rachel said.

Woody was wheeled into the cubicle just as Rachel pulled back the curtain, his face pale with pain. 'Oh, Suze, I'm so sorry. I've ruined our anniversary. I can't drive us to the hotel now. I'm not even sure I'll be able to go away.'

'Idiot,' she said, and kissed him. 'None of that matters. As long as I've still got you—I don't care about posh hotels and cocktails. It's *you* that's important. And thank God you're still here. When Baz phoned, it terrified the life out of me.'

Rachel had to swallow the lump in her throat. She'd found out the hard way that the posh hotels and cocktails had been more important to Steve than she was. Much as she would've liked to be loved the way that Suze Fleetwood clearly loved her husband, the idea of signing up for dating apps and putting herself out there felt way too daunting. How did you find love again when you were middle-aged? How did you deal with all the emotional baggage of a potential partner as well as your own?

Though, right now, she needed to concentrate on her patient's needs rather than her own insecurities. She introduced Dave to Mr Gupta, who talked him through the operation and answered as many questions as he could.

'I'm going to have a word with the anaesthetist and scrub in,' Mr Gupta said. 'Can you take Mr Fleetwood to Theatre Six, please?' he added to the porter.

'We can still have cocktails and bubbly at home, when you get out of hospital,' Suze said. 'And I'll cook you a steak, just the way you like it. Even if I have to cut it up for you and feed you like a baby.'

Woody gave her a watery smile. 'I love you, Suze.'

She kissed him. 'Love you, too. Always

have, always will.' She turned to Rachel. 'Thanks for doing what you've done, Doctor.'

'You're welcome,' Rachel said. 'All the best—and happy anniversary to you both.'

'Cheers, love,' Woody said. He was smiling again now, even though he was clearly worried sick; he'd definitely perked up as soon as his wife had arrived.

Suze held his good hand and walked alongside the trolley as the porter wheeled him out towards Theatre. And Rachel squashed the little sad bit of longing for a love like that in her own life, wrote up her notes, and went to find her next patient.

On Friday, when Rachel had finished writing up her notes before lunch, she headed for Tim's office. 'Busy?' she asked.

'Depends,' he said.

'Coffee and a sandwich? My shout, as you paid last time.'

'All right. And it'd be good to catch up and see how your first week's gone,' he said.

Once they were settled with lunch, he said, 'Right. Hit me with it. The good, the OK, and the things that need changing?'

'I love my colleagues, I love the team

spirit here, and Mr Gupta managed to save three out of my patient's four fingers from the other day—that's the excellent stuff. The paperwork's bearable and thank you for persuading HR to let me do the online stuff at home instead of dragging it out. And the things that need changing—well, the head of department would be all right if he kept his promise to introduce me to the best cheese shop in the world,' she said with a grin.

'That,' he said, 'can be arranged.'

'What are you doing on Saturday?' she asked.

'Laundry,' he said with a groan.

'Me, too. But can I tempt you out for an hour?'

He was silent for a moment, and she suddenly wondered if he thought she was hitting on him. 'As friends,' she added swiftly.

Was that relief she saw in his eyes? Either way, it was a reminder to her not to get too close to him.

'All right. I'll meet you at the Tube station at ten,' he said.

'Perfect,' she said, and switched the topic back to the safe topic of work. 'How's your head injury patient doing in ICU?'

'Holding his own,' he said. 'And your flail chest?'

'Discharged today. His wife popped in earlier with a tin of biscuits, a jar of coffee and a box of teabags for the staff room.'

'Ah, that's kind,' he said. 'But the bit I like best is hearing that someone who was rushed into us on a trolley is well enough to be discharged and go home.'

'Absolutely,' she agreed.

On Saturday, Tim waited outside the Tube station. Just friends, he reminded himself, feeling the little bubbles of excitement fizzing through his veins. Platonic friends, that was what they'd said they'd be. This wasn't the start of a relationship. He wasn't even looking for a relationship. But the bubbles of excitement increased as he saw her walking towards him. He lifted a hand in acknowledgement; as soon as she saw him, she smiled, and his heart felt as if it had done an anatomically impossible pirouette.

'Good morning, Mr Hughes.' Though she wasn't being formal in the slightest. She was being cheeky, and he liked her sense of fun.

He grinned. 'Good morning, Ms Halliday.

Ready for some intensely serious discussion about cheese?'

'Certainly am.'

He resisted the impulse to take her hand. Not appropriate, he reminded himself. But he chatted lightly to her on the way into the high street and realised how much he'd missed making inconsequential chatter with someone he felt instantly comfortable with. It was weird how it felt as if he'd known Rachel for years instead of for barely a week. They'd just clicked.

He led her through a couple of the back streets and stopped outside a shop. 'Ta-da.'

'Muzzy's Barn,' she said, reading the sign. 'OK.'

But as soon as they stepped inside, he heard her soft 'oh' of delight.

The cheese counter was dedicated to small artisanal cheeses; there were locally made chutneys, pickles, jams and jars of sauces; there was a deli section with a barrel of gleaming olives; there were artisanal bread and pastries, displayed beautifully; there were locally produced fruit, vegetables and eggs; and there was a section for locally roasted coffee and blended teas.

'It's like an indoor farmers' market,' she

said. 'And, look—they even have a specialist vegan section.' She smiled. 'My youngest is vegan. I'm definitely coming back here
and stocking up, before she's next due home.
There's some non-dairy cheese there I've
not seen before and it might have the right
texture.'

'I take it vegan cheese isn't a hit with
you?' he asked.

'Cashew-based soft cheeses are lovely,
and I've found something that's not far off
Camembert,' she said, 'but I've yet to find
something with the right texture to replace
a decent Cheddar.' She smiled. 'Though, actually, I've liked nearly all the things Saskia
and I have made together. I think our favourite's been the caponata sauce. And these,'
she added, taking a jar of capers off the shelf
and adding it to her basket, 'are so going in
the next batch I make.'

'So you like cooking?'

She nodded. 'And experimenting. Now
the girls are both at uni, my best friend's
my usual guinea pig.' She gestured to the
counter. 'My new second-best friend, if
he chooses, could be my guinea pig to say
thank you for introducing me to such a wonderful shop.'

She was inviting him to dinner as a friend and co-conspirator, not as a date. Which was a relief and a disappointment at the same time. 'I'd like that,' he said. 'But I'm afraid you get a choice of burned beans on charred toast or a takeaway in return. Hannah—my eldest—says I can't cook because I forget to keep an eye on things and can't follow a recipe. Which is a bit ridiculous, given that I can follow procedures to save a life. Her words, not mine.'

'I'd guess that work matters to you but cooking doesn't,' she said.

'Mandy did the cooking and I did the washing up,' he said. 'I'm guessing you had a similar arrangement?'

'We had a dishwasher,' she said, and looked away.

Her marriage had clearly been very different from his own close partnership. 'Sorry. I didn't mean to stomp over a sore spot.'

'It's fine,' she said. 'Let's go and look at the cheese.'

She seemed out of sorts, but he didn't know her well enough to know how to fix it. Being bright and breezy would be tantamount to sticking his fingers in his ears, closing his eyes and singing *La-la-la, I can't hear you.* Feeling awkward and cross with himself, he followed her to the cheese counter.

To his relief, she started talking with the young woman behind the counter about the different cheese, trying several; and then she turned to him to encourage him to do the same. By the time she'd added half a dozen different sorts to her basket, she was smiling again.

'Shall we stop and have a cup of coffee?' he suggested. 'The café here is very good.'

He wasn't surprised that she opted for the Parmesan shortbread to go with her coffee.

'This is seriously good,' she said after her first bite. 'I think it's as good as the cheese biscuits Mum taught me to make. I used to bake them for school fundraisers and family parties, and if people knew I was making them I'd get a bunch of texts begging for a doggie bag, so I always had to make an extra batch.'

'Sometimes the Emergency Department staff bring in things they've baked and leave them in the kitchen for everyone to share,' he said.

'Would that be a hint, Mr Hughes?'

'Just a teensy, tiny one,' he said.

She laughed. How pretty she looked when her eyes crinkled at the corners, he thought. Those were real laughter lines. Rachel Halliday might have had a rough couple of years, but she was definitely the sort of person who looked for the good in life.

'OK. Next time I do some baking, I'll bring them in,' she promised.

'I used to cheat,' he said, 'because Mandy used to make brownies for me to bring in. Nowadays I cheat and just buy a ton of brownies from the bakery down the road.'

'You don't fancy trying to make them yourself—burned baked beans aside? I have an easy one-step recipe—you just dump everything in a bowl and then mix it together.'

He shook his head. 'It'd just be a waste of ingredients. Baking isn't my thing.'

'I miss baking for school coffee mornings,' she said. 'And, as I'm an only child, I miss cooking big family meals. The Sunday roast, or the curry night. The nearest I get to it is batch-cooking a lasagne and putting individual portions in the freezer.' She smiled. 'Though Steve's family have told me I'm not getting away from them that easily and, in their view, I still count as part of them.'

'That's nice.' Thought he wasn't surprised that her ex's family wanted to keep her close. Rachel Halliday was lovely, the sort of woman whose smile made the day feel that little bit brighter. 'So what does my new second-best friend do on her days off?'

'Read, go for walks, maybe go to the cinema or the theatre—I don't mind going to see things on my own if nobody else fancies going with me,' she said. 'Sometimes I dance around the house, singing my head off to the old stuff. Oh, and I'm a bit of a crossword addict. What does my new second-best friend do?'

He'd been a hermit for the last couple of years, except for when his best friend or the girls had dragged him out. And he knew he spent too much time at work. It was easier to fill his head with paperwork that needed doing rather than face the emptiness of his house. He just hoped it would get better when Hannah was on maternity leave and he could do a bit of babysitting. 'I go to the odd gig,' he said. 'And I try to avoid dinner parties when I suspect I'm going to be set up with someone.' He paused. 'Maybe we could go for a walk together, some time.'

'I'd like that,' she said. She glanced at her

watch. 'And I need to stop taking up all your time.'

'The laundry's winning, now you've got your cheese?' he teased.

'Afraid so.' She smiled. 'I learned the hard way that it's easier to do things in smaller chunks; if you let them build up, they're a lot more daunting and take a lot more mental effort.'

'Good point. I, too, ought to do some laundry.' He couldn't quite bring himself to admit that he paid a cleaner to do his ironing as well as keep the house clean. It sounded too entitled.

'Thank you for bringing me here,' she said.

'My pleasure. I'd better let you go, as I need to pick up a couple more things while I'm in town,' he said. It wasn't actually true, but he didn't want her feeling obliged to offer to wander round the centre of Muswell Hill with him. Particularly as he was aware that he did actually want to spend more time with her, and that was a dangerous thing. He wasn't quite ready to move on from the past, and he had a feeling that it was pretty much the same for her. For both their sakes, it would be much more sensible to leave things be.

'I'll see you on Monday. Thanks for the coffee,' she said.

'My pleasure,' he said.

And oh, that smile. It warmed him all the way through and made him want to ask her to stay a bit longer. But that really wouldn't be a good idea. He had nothing to offer her; and he didn't want to make life complicated for either of them. So he smiled back and left the café.

CHAPTER THREE

RACHEL WAS ON a late shift on Monday; just after she'd started, an elderly man was brought in with a suspected AAA—an abdominal aortic aneurysm, which was a bulge in the main blood vessel running from the heart to the abdomen. As the swelling grew larger, the walls of the blood vessel grew thinner, and if the aneurysm ruptured the patient could bleed to death.

'This is a tricky one,' Samir, the paramedic who was doing the handover, said. 'John Reynolds, aged eighty-six. He had a fall this morning and he'd got pain in his lower back—the paramedics who saw him thought it was probably a fractured hip and took him in to his local hospital. No fracture, but they think it's an AAA. Apparently, he had a small one twenty-five years ago, but he took the advice to stop smoking, change his diet and start exercising, and according to him he's been fine ever since. He hasn't been on any medication at all, for the last seven years.'

Rachel raised her eyebrows. 'That's quite unusual, at his age.'

'I gather he's quite independent,' Samir said, 'and he doesn't think very much of his GP, which is why he refuses to go to appointments—he says he'll go to the walk-in centre if he has a problem. Anyway, he says he's been really well in himself, until he fell today.'

'Any history of falls?'

'According to him, no. Today was different because he tripped over the cat. Right now he's worried about his cat, he's got a pain in the middle of his tummy, and both legs hurt.'

'Got it. Any next of kin?'

'His daughter, Marnie. She's on her way here,' Samir said. 'And she says the neighbour's looking after the cat, so we can tell her dad not to worry. I've already told him, but I think he could do with the reassurance if you don't mind repeating it.'

'Of course,' Rachel said. 'Thanks, Samir.'

When Samir brought the patient in, Rachel introduced herself swiftly. 'Samir tells me you've had a fall and thought you'd broken your hip, Mr Reynolds, but the local hospital couldn't see anything on the X-ray and thought you might have an aneurysm.'

'I told them, that was twenty-five years ago now,' Mr Reynolds said. 'I'm fine.'

'What hurts?' she asked gently.

'My tummy, and both legs,' he said.

'Did you hit your head at all when you fell? Can you remember blacking out, even for a few seconds?'

'I might've hit my head, but I don't remember blacking out,' he said.

'Would you mind if I examined you and did a couple of tests?' she asked. When he gave his consent, she added, 'Marnie's on her way in, by the way, and she says to let you know that your neighbour's looking after your cat, so don't worry.'

'Smudge. He's a dear little thing. But he got under my feet, this morning—he was fretting, because I was late giving him his breakfast—and that's why I fell,' Mr Reynolds said. 'I felt such a fool. I couldn't get myself up again and I had to press my bracelet to get someone to come and help me.' He rolled his eyes. 'Marnie will say she told me so.'

'To be fair,' Rachel said, 'I used to worry about my mum having a fall. I made her wear a bracelet, too—that meant she could keep her independence and I wasn't worried sick about her all the time.'

'You girls worry too much.' He patted her hand. 'Tough as old boots, me.'

'Let's have a look,' she said.

But she really wasn't happy with the feel of his stomach; his blood pressure was lower than she would've liked, and his heart rate was too fast. There were definitely signs of a bleed, somewhere. 'I'm going to send you for a CT scan,' she said, 'just to give me a better idea of what's happening. And I'm going to take some bloods to check a couple of other things.'

When the blood tests results came back, she really wasn't happy. His blood wasn't clotting properly and the balance of acids and alkalis wasn't right. The CT scan showed a mass in the psoas muscle—the one in the back of the abdominal wall that went down the leg. The mass could be a cyst but, together with the other symptoms, she thought it was likely to be a haematoma. It wouldn't be an easy fix, because the muscle was hard to get to; plus there was a bleed on the brain that she wasn't happy about, either.

She headed for Tim's office. 'Got a couple of minutes?' she asked. 'I could do with a second pair of eyes on something.'

'Sure.'

She gave him a swift patient history and brought up the scan results on his screen. 'I'm thinking a psoas bleed, plus he hit his head when he fell and he's got a bleed there as well. And his bloods are all over the place.'

'I agree—that scan looks like a psoas bleed, and it's one for the surgical team,' he said. 'I think the best we can do is to sort his bloods here, if we can, and admit him to ICU for monitoring until the surgeons can get him on the table.'

By the time John Reynolds came back from his scan, he couldn't wiggle his toes and had no feeling in his feet or his right leg. Rachel's instincts were all on red alert: the symptoms meant that his peripheries were shutting down, and the bleed was getting more serious. She spoke to the surgical team and got him admitted to ICU. When his daughter arrived, Rachel took the time to explain what was happening and took her up to see her father. 'They'll have the most up-to-date information about how he's doing,' she said, 'and the surgeons will see you before they take your dad to Theatre.'

'He's done so well,' Marnie said. 'Most of his friends are gone, now, or are in nursing homes. That's why I suggested he adopted a cat, to give him a bit of company.' She bit her lip. 'I feel so guilty now. I can't believe he tripped over Smudge.'

'You couldn't have predicted the fall,' Rachel reassured her. 'And you'd persuaded him to wear an alarm on his wrist, so he could call for help, so you did the right thing there as well.'

Marnie nodded. 'I was panicking in case he'd fractured his hip and would have to go into a nursing home for months—he'd hate it, even though my neighbour works in one that's good and they'd look after him there as well as I would. But he's in better shape than some of *my* friends, and he can give most of them a good thirty years.'

'It's hard to lose your independence,' Rachel agreed. 'I felt really guilty about my mum going into a nursing home, but she needed more care than I could give her, and it was the best way to keep her safe. If your dad needs extra rehab after here, it won't be for a hugely long time. He'll cope—and, as you say, he'll have the cat for company when he gets back to his own place.' She just hoped that the surgeons could fix that bleed.

But, at the end of her shift, Theatre called down with the bad news: John hadn't made it off the operating table. Rachel could feel the tears pricking her eyelids. She forced herself to blink them away so she could deal with her last patient professionally, but by the time she'd changed out of her scrubs she was swallowing hard.

'Are you OK?'

She glanced up at Tim. 'Fine,' she fibbed.

He clearly wasn't buying it. 'What happened?'

'The patient I saw you about—he didn't make it.'

'I'm sorry.' He patted her shoulder awkwardly. 'You did your best for him. You did all the right things. A psoas bleed is hard to fix, and a bleed on the brain as well was a complication too many.'

She was incredibly aware of him. Where his hand had touched her shoulder, even though her scrubs had been a barrier between their skin, she tingled: which was crazy, not to mention inappropriate. Tim was her boss, and he was treating her in exactly the same way that he treated everyone else in the department. Ediye had told her that when they lost someone, Tim always squeezed their hands and reminded them that they'd done their best and they couldn't save everyone.

'Yeah, I guess,' she said.

'It's always hard when you lose a patient,' he said. 'But you've got nothing to reproach yourself about. We can't save everyone—we try to, but it's not humanly possible.'

'I know.' But it didn't stop her wishing she'd been able to fix things. Or that sudden longing to lean on him. For goodness' sake. She was an experienced doctor. She knew that some conditions just weren't fixable, and she didn't need to lean on anyone.

His blue eyes were filled with kindness—and was there something else, too, or was she deluding herself? 'See you tomorrow,' she said.

Though she was still out of sorts when she got home, both from losing her patient and from struggling with her inappropriate feelings towards Tim.

'He's your head of department,' she told herself out loud. Ha. As if that mattered. Plenty of people dated colleagues. 'And he's not looking for anything from you other than friendship. That's what you agreed. So stop thinking about him in any other sense.'

Despite her pep-talk, she couldn't get Tim Hughes out of her head. She liked him. More than liked him. But she didn't want to make a fool out of herself by making an unwanted move. Could she even trust her instincts any more? If she made a mistake, and what felt like mutual attraction really was nothing more than a platonic friendship, working together would be incredibly awkward.

Baking, when she got home, made her feel a bit better. The next morning, she left a box of the cheese biscuits in the staff kitchen, with a note.

Help yourself, from Rachel.

And she left a smaller box of them on Tim's desk with another short note.

Thanks for being kind yesterday. Enjoy, with best wishes from your second-best friend.

Tim was on a late and caught up with her just before her break. 'Those biscuits you left me: are they the ones you were telling me about? They're amazing.'

'I put some in the staff room as well,' she said, 'but I know how quickly they vanish at family get-togethers, so I gave you a separate box because I wanted to make sure my fellow cheese fiend did actually get some.'

'You,' he said, 'are a superstar. Thank you.'

Funny how his praise made her feel so warm inside.

On Friday afternoon, Tim sought her out in the office where she was filling out paperwork. 'Are you busy tonight?'

'I have a hot date,' she said, 'with the ironing.'

'I saw what you did there. Very good.' He laughed. 'Seriously, though, are you busy? I was going to a gig with my best friend tonight, but he's been called in to do some very tricky spinal surgery and he can't make it. It'd be a pity to waste the ticket.' He named a band she'd loved in her early twenties. 'They're playing a tiny gig in Camden, as a warm-up for their new tour. Would you like to come with me?'

'I'd love to,' she said. 'How much do I owe you for the ticket?'

'Nothing, because it would've just gone to waste.'

'Then maybe I can buy you a pizza and a beer first,' she suggested.

'All right, it's a deal.'

A deal, not a date, she reminded herself: even though she had that funny, fluttery feeling in her stomach when he smiled at her. 'Let me know what time it starts and where,' she said, 'and I'll find us a table somewhere nearby.'

She booked a pizza place near to the venue for an hour before doors opened and texted him with the details. When she got home after her shift, she reminded herself there was nothing romantic about this and she was simply going to a show with a friend; she dressed casually in jeans, low-heeled ankle boots and a plain black T-shirt that wouldn't make her feel sweaty in the heat of the club. Tim was already at the pizza place when she arrived, and raised his hand to greet her from their table; again, she had to ignore that funny fluttery feeling in her stomach.

She enjoyed chatting with him about music and was delighted to discover that they had quite a crossover in their tastes. They spent a while swapping tales about gigs they'd enjoyed and their favourite albums, and Rachel couldn't remember the last time she'd enjoyed herself so much.

In the venue, they managed to find their way to the front. The support band was good, and the main band was three songs into their set when some lads behind them decided they wanted to make a mosh pit, pushing into the crowd before them and swaying back again.

'We can move to the side away from them, if you want to,' Tim said. 'Or I can stand here as a buffer.' He frowned. 'I don't see why we should have to miss out just because they're being selfish.'

'I'm happy to do whatever you want,' she said.

Tim shifted so he was standing behind her, with one arm either side of her braced against the barrier to protect her from the worst of the shoving. It made her feel warm all the way through; Steve wouldn't have taken her to see the band in the first place, let alone acted so protectively, and she really appreciated how safe Tim made her feel.

Plus, if she was honest with herself, she

really liked having Tim's arms round her. It would be oh, so easy to let herself act on the attraction she felt towards him and let their relationship move past a simple friendship.

But was that what Tim wanted, too, or was he just being gentlemanly?

Asking was out of the question. She didn't want to risk making things awkward between them, either at work or as part of their new friendship. But she was aware of every movement he made, every brush of his body against hers.

After the gig, Tim saw Rachel home to Hampstead. She lived in a gorgeous period terraced house; he guessed that, like himself and Mandy, Rachel and her ex had bought the house years ago, before property prices had gone completely insane. He walked down the tiled path to the front door with her and waited while she extracted her key from her jeans pocket—all the while trying not to think about how well the soft denim hugged her curves.

'Thanks for—well, protecting me at the gig,' she said.

'You're very welcome. I'm only sorry that

those lads had to be selfish and spoil it for everyone else.'

'It's not your fault, and I still enjoyed myself. The music was great.' She gave him a slightly shy smile. 'Would you like to come in for coffee?'

If he had any sense, Tim thought, he'd say no and make the excuse that they had work tomorrow. He'd already got too close to Rachel tonight, standing at the gig with his arms round her. He'd done it primarily to protect her from the pushing of the lads behind them; but he'd enjoyed being close enough to her to feel the warmth of her body and breathe in the sweet vanilla scent she wore.

He opened his mouth to make the excuse, and a completely different set of words tumbled out, because his common sense clearly wasn't working in sync with his mouth. 'That'd be lovely.'

She opened the front door and ushered him in to a hallway with black and white chequered tiles.

'This house is too big for just me. I'm kind of rattling around in it,' she said. 'But I'm not planning to downsize until both the girls have finished uni and are settled. I want to make sure they always have a home.'

He nodded. 'I know what you mean. Mandy and I kept dithering about downsizing, once the girls had graduated, and then we decided we needed room for any future grandchildren to come and stay. I'm kind of glad we did, especially now Hannah's going to have her first baby, but being the only person in a family home feels a bit...' He wrinkled his nose. 'As you say, rattling around.' And he wasn't ready to lose all the memories, starting over in a new home.

'The room on the left was Mum's room,' she said, gesturing to a door in the hallway. 'It's the guest room, now. The girls and I painted it over the summer. There's a bathroom en-suite, so if you need the loo that's probably the quickest, or there's a bathroom up the stairs and straight in front of you.'

She led him past the door on the right, which he assumed led to the living room, and through to the kitchen. There was a beech dining table with six chairs on one side of the room, in front of large French doors; the kitchen cabinets were all cream, and there was a pine dresser with blue glassware and pretty china cups and saucers on display. The room was tidy and the work surfaces uncluttered; there was a vase of flowers on the windowsill, next to a narrow tray which held three terracotta pots full of fresh herbs.

'Would you prefer coffee or tea?' she asked.

'Coffee, please—decaf, if you have it, and just a splash of milk.'

'I stick to decaf at this time of night, too,' she said, taking a jar from the fridge then shaking grounds into a cafetière.

'What, no posh coffee machine?' he teased.

'No—not when all the pods end up in landfill,' she said. 'This is a bit old-fashioned, but it works just fine, and I can save the grounds for mulch in the garden.'

'My girls have nudged me into a few eco changes, over the years,' he said. 'I can't quite bear to give up my coffee machine, but Sophie found these metal pods that you fill yourself, wash up and reuse rather than dump in the trash.'

'That's a good idea,' she said. 'I might look into doing that.'

He noticed the photographs held to the

outside of the fridge with magnets. 'Can I be nosey?'

'Sure.'

There were photographs of Rachel with two girls who were clearly her daughters, and others with an older woman who looked so like her that it was obviously her mum. There was another snap with the four of them in front of a Christmas tree; Rachel and her mother were wearing Santa hats, the girls were sporting hairbands with reindeer antlers, and they were all laughing and holding up a glass of something bubbly.

'We took that one the Christmas before last,' she said, 'when Mum could still join in.'

Two Christmases ago. It had been his first Christmas without Mandy, and he'd made sure that he was working a split shift so he was too busy to even think about what he was missing. Then he'd gone home and curled up in a bed that was way too wide and, knowing nobody would see, sobbed his eyes out for an hour.

Last Christmas had been rough, too. He'd worked a double shift to block it out.

This Christmas... He was dreading it. The misery and the memories and the loss, bound together with the guilt that he wasn't there enough for his girls. But working was the only way he knew how to keep everything from battering his heart. He could block out his feelings with work. He'd rather patch up the drunks who'd lost their temper and ended up in a family fight than ruin Christmas for either of his daughters by sitting brooding in a corner. Yet, at the same time, he felt guilty for not being there enough for them.

It looked as if Rachel loved Christmas as much as Mandy had. He'd bet she would make a traditional wreath for the door with her daughters, just as Mandy had, and put up a real tree, scenting the air with pine. The fir tree that Mandy had nurtured and brought in every year had remained outside for the last couple of years, completely neglected. Tim hadn't even been able to face putting up a small artificial tree, let alone decorating it, and he'd left all the Christmas cards in a heap on the sideboard rather than pegging them up on a string over the door.

He didn't know what to say. Part of him wanted to run and avoid any discussion about Christmas; yet part of him wanted to stay. Could Rachel help him see things differently and find a way back to all the warmth and the wonder?

As if she'd guessed what was going on in his head, she handed him a mug of coffee. 'Let's go and sit down.'

'Thank you.'

Not Christmas, he decided as he sat at the table opposite her. Think about anything except Christmas and all the happiness he'd taken for granted would carry on and on and on—but had abruptly stopped.

He stared out of the patio doors. Of course. He couldn't see it in the dark, but there was obviously a garden out there. And she'd said earlier about keeping her coffee grounds as mulch. This would be a safe topic of conversation. 'Are you much of a gardener?'

'Not really,' she admitted. 'The garden's mostly shrubs because one of my ex's friends started a landscape gardening business years ago and we asked him to design us something low-maintenance and child-friendly.' She smiled. 'And thankfully he comes back every autumn to prune everything for us and sort anything out that isn't quite working. But I've got also little clumps of spring bulbs from pots that the girls bought me over the years, and I planted out when they'd stopped flowering. The troughs on the patio are a bit bare at the moment, but in the summer they're full of wildflowers; it helps to bring the butterflies and bees into the garden.' She looked at him. 'Are you a gardener, then?'

'I'm not much of anything, really,' he said. Apart from being a workaholic. 'We have a few roses and things in the garden.' Things he'd neglected horribly, along with the fir tree, because nothing had felt right without Mandy.

'It's hard to find the time to do everything,' she said. 'I've learned not to beat myself up about it. With a job as demanding as ours, something has to give.' She chuckled. 'With me, it's the oven. I pay someone to clean it for me. And my living room only really gets a dusting and a proper hoovering when I know someone's coming over, because the kitchen is my favourite room in the house and it's where I spend most of my time.'

'It's a nice room,' he said. Warm. Comfortable. Inviting.

'The French doors and the windows make it really light in the daytime,' she said. 'And I'm not a big one for telly. I'd rather

sit here with a mug of tea and read or listen to music.'

'That sounds good to me.' Tim was relieved that she'd managed to get his head to
change gear; but she'd also given him something to think about.

*I've learned not to beat myself up about
it... Something has to give.*

She was right. He was struggling—and
he'd been struggling for a long time. Maybe
it was time he admitted it, instead of beating
himself up about it or trying to block it out
with work. But the words stuck in his throat.

He finished his coffee and lifted his mug.
'I'll wash this up before I go.'

'No need,' she said, taking it from him.

'And I'd better let you get some sleep.
Thank you for coming with me tonight.'

'Thank you for asking me. I really enjoyed it.'

He honestly meant to just kiss Rachel's
cheek, as he would with any of his and Mandy's joint friends. But somehow his lips
ended up touching the corner of her mouth.
She froze. He was about to pull away and
apologise, when she moved closer, and her
lips brushed against his.

His mouth tingled where her lips touched

his. The next thing he knew, they were really kissing; his arms were wrapped round her waist and hers were wrapped round his neck. And there was a warmth spreading through him, as if a long, icy, lonely winter had finally ended and spring was starting to break through.

He broke the kiss and rested his forehead briefly against hers. 'I'm sorry. That really wasn't meant to happen.'

'It hadn't been my intention, either,' she said. 'I know neither of us is looking for a relationship.'

'This thing between us was meant to be strictly friendship,' he said.

'It's what we agreed. I kept telling myself the same.' She rested her palm against his cheek, and her grey eyes were huge and serious. 'Except, if I'm honest, I *like* you, Tim. And I liked it when you put your arms round me at the gig tonight to protect me.'

If she could be honest about it, so could he. 'Me, too. I mean, about liking you. And about liking holding you tonight at the gig. It just felt right, being close to you.' He bit his lip, aware that neither of them had moved; his arms were still wrapped round her waist and hers were round his neck. 'So what do we do now? Pretend this didn't happen?'

'Right now,' she said drily, 'you couldn't get a blade of grass between us, so we can't exactly deny it's happening.'

'There is that,' he admitted. But where did they go from here? What did she want? What did *he* want? He wasn't sure. This whole thing scared and thrilled him at the same time. 'What do we do?' he asked.

'I don't know,' she said. 'Maybe I'm a bit set in my ways, but the whole idea of starting all over again, at the age of fifty-two, terrifies me. I don't even know where to begin dating again. How do you even meet someone?' She shook her head. 'I know there are internet dating sites, but how do you know people are telling the truth on their profiles? And going to a speed-dating evening or what have you just isn't my thing.'

'I've never done it. But I imagine it's like being on parade, pretending to be someone you're not, and being judged by people who don't know you.' He grimaced. 'Which sounds even worse than the set-up dates.'

'At least your friends *know* the people they're trying to set you up with and can reassure you that you've really got something in common, and that they're nice,' she agreed. She looked at him. 'So what happens now?'

He wanted to date her. At the same time, the idea made him antsy. What if it went wrong? Working together would be awkward. And what if it went right? Would that mean wiping Mandy completely out of his life?

As if she guessed what he was thinking—or, more likely, she had similar doubts—she said, 'Just so we're clear, if things do happen between us, I'm not trying to replace Mandy.'

'Thank you,' he said. 'And I'm not trying to replace your ex.' He paused. 'I really like you, Rachel, and I don't want to wreck what could be a really good friendship. But, at the same time, I think there's something else between us. Can we keep things low profile for now, until we've worked out where this thing between us is going and what we both want from it?'

'That's a really good idea.'

He kissed her. Just because he could. He'd almost forgotten what it felt like to kiss someone, and he really liked the feel of Rachel's mouth against his. 'Is it weird that I feel like a teenager again?'

'No,' she said, 'because so do I. Though I haven't dated anyone else since I met Steve, nearly a quarter of a century ago, and I don't have a clue what dating etiquette is, nowadays.'

Neither did he.

'What about the set-up dates?' he asked.

'They don't count,' she said, 'because if I accept an invitation to go and see my friends it isn't the same thing as accepting a date to have dinner with someone I've only just met.'

'I haven't dated anyone else since I met Mandy, which is even longer ago,' he said. 'So don't expect me to be smooth and suave and sophisticated.'

She laughed. 'I promise, as long as you don't expect me to be a siren.'

He gave her an assessing look. 'You have siren potential.'

'Honestly? I'd rather be in jeans and boots and a big sweater, out for a long walk, than wearing high heels and a slinky dress at a cocktail party.'

'Me, too. Walks rather than cocktail parties, that is.' He rubbed the tip of his nose against hers. 'Are you off on Sunday?'

'Yes.'

'So am I. I'm going to my daughter Hannah's for dinner in the evening but, if it's not raining, how do you fancy a walk in Richmond Park on Sunday morning to see the deer? Maybe grab some lunch while we're out?'

'Going with the flow? That,' she said, 'sounds wonderful. Even if it rains, we can still go and see the deer; we'll just need to remember an umbrella and waterproof coats.'

'Great.' He kissed her again. 'I'll see you on Sunday. Shall I meet you here?'

'You live in Muswell Hill, right?'

He nodded.

'Then let's meet at Hampstead Heath station, because there's a direct overground train from there to Richmond.'

'All right. I'll see you on Sunday at Hampstead Heath station,' he confirmed. 'What time?'

'Quarter past nine?' she suggested.

'Perfect. See you then.' He stole a last kiss. 'Sweet dreams.'

CHAPTER FOUR

SUNDAY MORNING WAS Rachel's first 'first date' in nearly a quarter of a century, and she wasn't sure whether she was more excited or apprehensive about it. Part of her was dying to tell her best friend about it; but on the other hand she and Tim had agreed to keep this just between them, for now. Which made sense. If things went wrong, then Jenny would see the fact that Rachel had actually dated someone as the green light to set her up with someone else—whereas if things went wrong, she'd want a lot more time to regroup.

Despite what she'd told Tim about being more comfortable in jeans than in a cocktail dress, she made an effort with her hair and actually wore lipstick. She glanced out of the window, noting that it was frosty outside, and opted to wear her walking boots, slipping an umbrella into the pocket of her waterproof jacket.

Tim was waiting for her outside the train station. 'Hi.' He greeted her with a smile, then bent to kiss her cheek.

'Hi.' And it suddenly didn't matter that it was cold and damp and grey. It felt as if the sun had come out. Just being with him made the day feel brighter.

He held her hand all the way on the train to Richmond, and on the bus to Richmond Park itself. It was sweet and cherishing and endearing, all at the same time.

'It's the perfect autumn day,' he said. 'I love this time of year, when it's frosty and a bit misty, and you can crunch through the leaves.'

'"Seasons of mist and mellow fruitfulness",' she quoted. 'I used to love taking the girls to the park, all wrapped up in scarves and gloves and coats, and we'd look for conkers.'

'So did we. It feels like five minutes ago and twenty years, all at the same time,' he said. 'Let's head this way and see if we can find the deer.'

He held her hand as they walked through the park, too. If anyone had told Rachel when

she was fifteen that it was just as thrilling
to hold hands with someone in your fifties
as it was when you were in your teens, she
would never have believed them; yet it really
was just as heady and exciting. She could
feel the blood thrumming through her veins
and butterflies in her stomach. It was crazy.
She hadn't been looking for a relationship.
And she definitely didn't want to repeat the
heartache she'd felt after Steve's final be-
trayal. Yet at the same time, she was enjoying the anticipation and excitement of a first
date: those fizzy, sparkly feelings about all
the possibilities opening up before her.

The sun finally broke through the clouds,
dispelling the mist and turning the frosted
grass and bracken into glittering silver
where its rays shone through the branches of
the almost bare trees. Here and there, the last
few leaves hung from the branches in shades
of yellow and copper and ruby, the colours
bright against the darkness of wet bark;
fallen leaves had drifted like copper snow
beneath the trees. It was the most gorgeous
late autumn morning; then they rounded a
corner and saw a red stag standing in the
bracken, his head lifted and his antlers looking as if they were crowning him.

'Oh, look at him! He's beautiful. So majestic.' Rachel took her phone from her pocket and took a few snaps of the deer at a safe distance.

A second deer came to join the first, and then a third and fourth, the colour of their coats almost blending with the bracken; the females grazed with the stag looking over them, and Rachel stood watching them, with Tim's arms wrapped round her and his cheek pressed against hers.

'Aren't they stunning? This is the perfect Sunday morning,' he whispered against her ear. Then he kissed the spot just behind her ear and sent desire licking up her spine. She couldn't remember the last time she'd felt that heady, powerful need to kiss someone. Part of her worried that she was rushing into things, but the impulse to kiss him was too strong; she turned round in his arms so she could kiss him thoroughly.

When she broke the kiss, they were both shaking.

'I think a whole herd could've stomped past us, just now, and we wouldn't have noticed,' he said huskily.

She stroked his face. 'You're telling me.'

* * *

Was this weird, long-forgotten feeling blooming through him happiness? Tim wondered. He'd spent the last two and a half years burying himself in work, keeping himself too busy to think and to feel. But with Rachel, he was content. Something as simple as walking through the park, enjoying the autumn landscape and each other's closeness, had made him feel so much brighter.

His first proper date since he'd lost Mandy.

And there was something about Rachel Halliday that drew him, that made him want to step out of the shadows with her and seize the brightness. Maybe this could be his second chance. And this time he'd try harder to get it right, to balance his work and his life a bit better and reconnect properly with his daughters.

But in the meantime, he was going to live in the moment. Enjoy the gorgeous surroundings of the park with someone who noticed things, but who didn't feel the need to fill every moment with chatter. The more time he spent with Rachel, the more he liked her.

By lunchtime, they'd walked up an appetite; they found the café and loaded their trays with hot soup, fresh bread and a shared bowl of rosemary salted chips.

Rachel smiled as they sat down at one of the tables. 'Jenny would be nagging us about our salt intake if she saw this. But I think that hot, crispy chips *need* salt.'

'Agreed—plus we have wholemeal bread and vegetable soup, which is good for our gut biome,' Tim said. 'I reckon that cancels out the chips.'

'Good point,' she said.

There was a dimple in her cheek when she smiled; it was so, so cute. He smiled at her. 'I was wondering what made you decide to become a doctor?'

'I wanted to be a nurse or a doctor right from when I was tiny,' she said. 'I was always bandaging my teddy bears when I was a toddler, and my favourite Christmas present ever was a doctor's kit from my godmother. I used to take everyone's pulse and pretend to listen to their heart through my stethoscope.'

He could just imagine that.

'I was lucky,' she said. 'Mum always championed me, even though it was a bit of a struggle for money for me to go to university.'

'What about your dad?'

She shook her head. 'He hasn't been in my life for a very long time.'

Tim winced. 'I'm sorry. I didn't mean to bring up difficult memories.'

'Not a problem,' she said. 'I was lucky in having the best mum in the world. I have no regrets. So how about you? What made you want to be a doctor?'

'I was fascinated by science when I was at school,' he said. 'You know, all the kitchen science experiments—the vinegar and baking soda volcano, making a battery for a clock with a potato and zinc and copper wire, that sort of thing. My gran had been a chemist, so she encouraged me to do the experiments. But then she died from a heart attack when I was about ten. I missed her hugely, and it made me want to be a doctor, so I could save other people from having to lose their grans.'

'But you chose emergency medicine rather than cardiology?'

'The emergency department was my favourite rotation, in my houseman years,' he said. 'I like the mad pace, and the fact that we can actually see the difference we make to people's lives. What made you pick emergency medicine?'

'It was pretty tough to choose between emergency medicine and obstetrics,' she said. 'I really loved bringing a new life into the world, those first moments when you look into a baby's eyes and see all the wonder. But even more than that I love being able to save someone's life, being able to give people hope when they'd been expecting the worst.'

'There's nothing like it,' he agreed.

'Was anyone in your family a medic?' she asked.

He shook his head. 'As I said, Gran was a chemist, but it was industrial rather than pharmaceutical. I come from a long line of lawyers. That's what I was supposed to be, too—especially as I was my dad's only son. Even though my older sister has made a much better lawyer than I would ever have been, he wasn't very happy when I sat him down and explained that I wanted to be a doctor and I wasn't going to follow in his footsteps. I don't think he ever forgave me.' He smiled wryly. 'I always felt I was a disappointment to him, and I guess that's one of the reasons I worked so hard early on—I wanted to make him proud of me.' He shrugged. 'I guess it became a bit of an ingrained habit, and I carried on. Though I swore I'd never be like him with my girls—whatever they wanted to do, I'd support them and make sure they knew they'd always have my backing.'

'What do they do?'

'Hannah, my eldest, is an English teacher; she followed in her mum's footsteps. She's about to start maternity leave.'

'When's the baby due?' she asked.

'The middle of December,' he said.

'A Christmas baby. How lovely.' She smiled. 'Christmas will be really special for you, this year,' she said.

Tim had been blocking that out, because he had no idea how he was going to cope with it. He found Christmas hard enough as it was. Adding his first grandchild as well, a reminder of all the things he couldn't share with Mandy any more...

But Rachel had asked him about his daughters, and he didn't want her to notice that he was brooding. 'Sophie, my youngest, has set up her own digital marketing consultancy for small businesses. Don't ask me what she actually does, because she talks about stuff I really don't understand,' he said. Hoping to head the conversation far away from Christmas, he asked, 'What about your girls?'

'Meg's reading music in Manchester. She's already sorted out a place for her PGCE next September because she wants to teach music—the subject, that is, not an instrument.'

'What does she play?' he asked.

'Piano and guitar, though actually she can play any instrument she picks up. I think she's good enough to make a living professionally, but she says hardly anyone makes a decent living as a musician, and she doesn't want to be a session musician. She'd rather have a settled job in teaching and play in a band on the side for fun.'

'It sounds as if she's very sensible and practical,' Tim said. A lot like Rachel herself.

'She is,' Rachel said.

'What about your younger daughter?'

'Saskia's at Sheffield, reading biochemistry. She wants to work in a research lab and save the world—I think she'll do it, too, because she has a huge heart.'

Also like Rachel herself, Tim thought.

The more he was getting to know her, the more he liked her.

They went for another wander through the park, and then Tim saw Rachel back to her house and kissed her goodbye on the doorstep.

'You're very welcome to come in,' she said.

'It's kind of you to ask,' he said, 'but Hannah's expecting me.' Part of him was tempted to ask Rachel to come with him; he knew his daughter wouldn't mind. On the other hand, he didn't want to rush this—and a selfish part of him wanted to keep Rachel to himself for a little longer. 'I'll see you tomorrow at work,' he said, 'and maybe we can go to the cinema in the week? I don't mind what we see, though I'm not a huge fan of gory stuff.'

'Me neither,' she said. 'I was planning to go and see that new comedy drama—the one that's been tipped for several awards.'

'I'd quite like to see that, too,' he said.

She smiled. 'All right. I'll check the listings and book something. Which evening's good for you?'

'I'm on early shifts Tuesday, Wednesday

and Thursday,' he said, 'so any of those work for me.'

'OK. I'll sort it out and let you know,' she said.

Another date. Part of Rachel worried that this wasn't a good idea. She wasn't looking for a permanent relationship, and her experiences with Steve had made her wary of trusting her heart to anyone else. On the other hand, she liked what she'd seen of Tim, and she wanted to get to know him better. And it would be nice to see a film with someone else, so they could chat about it afterwards.

In the end, she booked tickets for the Thursday evening.

'Do you want to grab something to eat, first?' Tim asked.

'I thought we could eat at the cinema,' she said.

'There's a café?'

'Not exactly. Instead of normal cinema seats, they have sofas with tables, so you place your order on their app, and the staff bring the food and drink to your table,' she explained.

'What a great idea,' Tim said. 'As you

bought the tickets, I'll buy the food and drink.'

They shared several dishes between them and a bottle of Pinot Grigio, and Rachel thoroughly enjoyed the film. And most of all she enjoyed holding hands with Tim all the way through the second half: being with someone who was actually present, instead of checking his phone every five minutes.

As the screening finished reasonably early, Tim suggested having coffee at his place.

'I'd love to,' she said.

They chatted about the film all the way on the Tube and then as they walked to Tim's house. He led them down a tiled pathway to a large Edwardian terraced house with a large bay window.

'It needed a bit of work when we bought it, but it had so many original features and we fell in love with those,' he said. 'Those six-over-two panes in the windows, the spandrels in the porch, and the leaded lights in the door.'

'It looks lovely,' she said.

'Let me give you the guided tour,' he said, opening the front door. 'Hallway, obviously.' The hallway had its original geometric tiled flooring, with the wooden panelling beneath the dado rail painted a soft dove grey, and the wall above painted cream. He gestured to a door on the left. 'Obviously the downstairs toilet isn't original, though we went for Edwardian-style fittings when we could afford it.' He led her through the first door. 'Living room.' The walls were painted Wedgwood blue, with cream paintwork; there was a huge mirror over the original cast-iron fireplace, and overstuffed bookshelves either side of the chimney breast. There was a large geometric-patterned rug on the polished floorboards, and the navy sofas with their cushions embroidered in jewel-like colours looked incredibly comfortable. It would be the perfect reading nook, she thought.

There was a collection of photo frames along the mantelpiece. 'Can I be nosey?' she asked.

'Sure.'

The photos were a similar mix to the ones in her own house: Tim's wedding to Mandy, graduation photos of themselves with their own parents and then with their daughters, and a couple of what were clearly much-loved candid family snaps taken in the garden or on holiday. She could see that Tim's daughters had inherited his dark hair and cornflower-blue eyes rather than Mandy's blonde hair and lighter blue eyes. And they seemed a warm, close, loving family— much like she'd tried so hard to make her own to be.

'Mandy looks a really lovely person,' she said. There was a sunniness about her in the photographs that made Rachel think they would've been friends, if they'd ever met.

'She was,' Tim said. 'But I'm not comparing you to her. You're very different. Both lovely, in your own ways.'

Rachel smiled. 'I wasn't fishing for a compliment.'

'I know. But it's kind of awkward…' He tailed off.

She knew what he meant: his very new girlfriend seeing photographs of his late wife. Yet this was still very early days between them; and she'd never been the jealous type. Right now, there was nothing to be jealous about. And, even if it did work out between them, she believed that hearts expanded and there would be room in his life for both herself and his memories of Mandy. 'It's fine. I've always thought that feelings aren't like a piece of cake where you have to grab the plate back and chop off a corner to give to someone else.'

'Because then all you'd be able to offer someone is a pile of crumbs,' he said.

'I'd be more concerned if you'd put all the photos away in a box and were pretending that Mandy never existed. I still have a couple of framed photos in the house with Steve, the girls and me, because there were some good times as well as the rough bits. At the end of the day, he's still their dad and I don't want to cut him out of their lives.' Her ex was doing a good enough job of that by himself, she thought.

'Fair point. This is obviously the dining room,' he said as he took her through to the next room. The walls were painted sage-green; again there was cream paintwork and polished floorboards, an original cast-iron and tiled fireplace, and there was a large table in the centre with eight chairs. The curtains were a green Morris print; there was a reproduction of Monet's *Water Lily Pond* on one wall, and another of two little girls in a garden of lilies.

'John Singer Sargent,' he said, noticing her gaze. 'Mandy loved that painting since the moment she first saw it in the Tate. I bought her a proper art print, and had it framed for her birthday a few years back.'

'It goes really well with this room,' she said.

'Yeah.' He took her through to the kitchen. 'Mandy was the cook. I'm afraid I just shove stuff in the microwave or the toaster,' he said with a wry smile, 'and even then, you can't assume that I checked the toaster settings before I shoved the bread in.'

It was the kind of kitchen that cried out to be the hub of a family home, with its grey-painted cabinets and beech work-tops and a matching table and chairs at one end. Though it looked more like a show-room kitchen than one that was used, Rachel thought; there were no herbs or plants growing on the windowsill, and there wasn't so much as a newspaper on the table. There was a calendar on the wall, but there were no dates filled in, and she noticed that the page on display was still that of the previous month. Rachel could've wept for him; it was obvious that he was lost without the centre of his family.

He took her through to the final room, which led off the kitchen. 'This is the garden room. We had it built when the girls were teenagers, though we did re-use the original back door.' The wall that wasn't glass had been painted cream, with a large clock set on it, and the whole thing was light and airy. There was a large potted palm in one corner, and an oversized clock on the wall; fairy lights were draped artfully round the window frames and the top of the painted wall, and the sofa and chairs looked incredibly comfortable, piled with cushions. She could imagine his girls here with their friends, just as her daughters would've been: mugs of coffee on the table and music playing as a background to chatter and laughter.

'Righty. I promised you coffee.' He led her back to the kitchen. 'Take a seat.' He measured coffee into a metal gadget she assumed was the reusable pod he'd told her about and set the machine running while he took two mugs from the cupboard.

'Tell me about Mandy,' she said.

'We met at uni. Mandy was doing her teacher training year, and I was in my last year—I was a year older than her,' he said. 'We were both out with a group of friends. Someone jostled her at the bar, and she ended up spilling the best part of a glass of red wine over me.'

'A bit of a different way to meet,' she said with a smile; though she was pretty sure that Tim would have laughed it off rather than having had a hissy fit about wine spilling over his clothes.

'She asked if she could take me for a pizza, the next night, to apologise for covering me in wine. I said she didn't need to apologise, but I liked the way she smiled so I said yes to the pizza, and we'd go halves on the bill.' He looked wistful. 'We just clicked, and we talked for hours, that night. We just didn't notice the time, and the staff ended up having to ask us to leave because they wanted to close the restaurant.' He smiled. 'We got married just after we graduated. The first year was a bit tough—you know what junior doctor hours are like, and it was her first year as a secondary school teacher—but we got through it. We were a team. The plan was that she'd make assistant head of department and I'd be a registrar before we started trying for children—but Hannah had other ideas and made her appearance a year or so earlier than we'd expected.' His face softened. 'Becoming a dad—I thought I knew it all, being a medic. I mean, I'd even delivered a baby. But nothing prepared me for how it felt when I looked into our little girl's eyes for the first time. That rush of love just blew me away. And it was the same when Soph arrived. I'm not one to cry in public, but I bawled my eyes out when I first held them,' he confessed. 'And both our girls have been brilliant, this last couple of years.'

'The perfect family?' she asked lightly.

'No, a *normal* family,' he corrected. 'We don't always agree on things. Mandy and I used to row over me working too hard, and I admit I missed most of the girls' sports days.' He wrinkled his nose. 'I was late for parent-teacher evening a few times, but I never missed one of their performances— whether it was one of the girls singing "Twinkle, Twinkle, Little Star" at an end-of-term nursery school concert, right through to Hannah playing Lady Macbeth in sixth form and doing the whole "out, damn'd spot" bit. I was always there, as near to the front as I could get, and made sure they could see me clapping and cheering them on. We used to take them out for dinner after the performance to make a fuss of them and tell them how proud we were of them.'

Meg and Saskia couldn't say the same about their own dad, Rachel thought with a pang. Two times out of three, Steve had found an excuse why he couldn't make it to a school performance, and he'd almost never made parent-teacher evenings, saying that Rachel was much better at dealing with them than he was. Only now, with the benefit of hindsight, had Rachel realised it hadn't been work keeping him away: it had been a stolen date with his latest mistress.

Tim put a mug of coffee in front of her.

She took a sip. 'This is perfect,' she said. 'Thank you.'

'My pleasure.' He opened a tin marked *Biscuits* and wrinkled his nose. 'Stale digestives. Not the sort of thing you should offer a guest.' Then he rummaged in a cupboard and emerged waving a packet of biscuit curls, which he decanted onto a plate. 'I hoped I still had these. I'll replace them before Hannah drops round next—it's her latest pregnancy craving,' he said.

Tim Hughes was definitely the sort of man who'd notice something like that and act on it, she thought, touched. The little things added up and made a lot.

'Tell me about Steve,' he said.

'We met at a party when I was doing my last year as a house officer,' she said. 'He was a friend of a friend. He worked in advertising, so he had the gift of the gab and a boatload of charm—and the most soulful brown eyes. You know how it's impossible to resist a spaniel?' At Tim's nod, she continued, 'It was like that with him. One look and I'd just melt. And he made me laugh. I thought I'd found my perfect partner. We'd been together for almost a year when he took me to this little café opposite the Eiffel Tower for breakfast. I'd ordered an almond croissant, and it came out on a plate with *Veux-tu m'épouser?* written in chocolate beside it, and on top of the croissant there was a tiny paper case with a solitaire diamond nestled in it.'

It was nothing like Tim's own proposal to Mandy on a beach in Northumbria, when they'd gone for a walk, got totally drenched in an unexpected rainstorm, and he'd apologised but she'd just laughed off the fact that they were both soaked and freezing. That moment, he'd realised she was the one he wanted to spend the rest of his life with, and he'd asked her to marry him. No ring, no witnesses, nobody to document the moment. Just the two of them, a kiss and a promise they'd both kept until she'd died.

Then he realised Rachel was waiting for him to respond. 'Very romantic,' he said, trying to be diplomatic. Though if she wanted grand, flashy gestures from him, she'd end up very disappointed. That wasn't who he was.

'It did kind of sweep me off my feet. I said yes. And I thought we were happy,' she said. 'Steve was working his way up the ladder at work, so he had to put the hours in; and, as you said, there's never any time when you're a junior doctor because you're always on call. But then I fell pregnant with Meg, and I had really hideous morning sickness. Not quite hyperemesis but getting on that way.' She paused. 'That was when he had his first affair.'

Tim stared at her, shocked. His *first* affair? That meant her husband must've had more than one fling. And the timing, when Rachel had been so vulnerable, pregnant and suffering with morning sickness... Even though he knew it was none of his business, he couldn't help asking, 'Why did you stay with him?'

'I was going to leave him,' Rachel said. 'I talked it over with Mum, hoping that she'd let me come back to stay with her until I could find a flat for me and the baby. But she'd been there, too. When she found out my father was actually working his way through her friends, she left him. But her parents were from the generation who didn't believe in divorce—they said she'd made her bed, so she had to lie on it.'

'Harsh,' Tim said.

She nodded. 'My dad was about as reliable at seeing me and making maintenance payments as he was at being faithful, so we struggled a lot when I was little. Mum didn't want my life to be as tough as hers had been, and she talked me round. The way she saw it, being a single mum is really difficult. Not just financially, but the fact that you're the one who has to make all the decisions, and you haven't got anyone to share the worries with, or anyone who can take over and let you sleep when you're bone-deep tired and terrified of letting yourself drift off in case you're sleeping so heavily you don't wake when the baby cries. And she persuaded me that maybe Steve had made a mistake because I'd had a tough pregnancy and he simply wasn't coping with seeing me so poorly and knowing he couldn't really do anything to help me.'

Tim didn't think that was anywhere near a good enough excuse, but it wasn't his place to say so.

'Except,' she said quietly, 'Steve did exactly the same thing when I was pregnant with Saskia. For him it was more of a three-year itch than a seven-year itch. He was good with the girls when they were little, and I wanted them to grow up in a stable home rather than waiting for a dad who never turned up, the way I had, so I put up with it.' She grimaced. 'I always knew when he'd started an affair, because he'd be late home all the time and suddenly start having to work weekends at the office; and I always knew when it ended because he'd be back to being home at a normal time and he'd bring me flowers every Friday night.'

Tim had always brought Mandy flowers on a Friday night: not because he'd had a guilty conscience, but because he knew how much she loved fresh flowers and he'd liked to see the pleasure in her eyes when he gave them to her. It had been one of the little rituals that helped cement a marriage.

'Looking back now, I guess I'd always known that Steve was selfish, but in the early years I managed to justify it to myself,' Rachel said. 'He had a high-pressure job.'

And a doctor in the emergency department had a low-pressure job? Tim didn't ask the question, but he felt cross on her behalf.

'He was busy at work.'

That went for doctors, too. Tim's crossness intensified. 'So I guess you wish you hadn't listened to your mum?' he asked.

'Sort of,' she said, 'though Mum did give me one really solid bit of advice: to keep my money separate from Steve's and have a joint account just for bills. She'd had money when she got married to my dad, but everything had been in their joint account, and he cleaned her out when she left him.' She gave him a wry smile. 'Steve was almost as bad with money as my dad was. He liked designer clothes and very posh restaurants. When he bought me flowers, the bouquets were always really fancy ones from an expensive florist. I always felt so bad about him spending so much money on something so frivolous; I would much rather have had a cheap bunch of daffodils or what have you and given the rest of the money to charity.'

Oh. So she *didn't* like flashy gestures. Tim was relieved. 'So what made you finally leave him?'

'I didn't. He left me,' Rachel said. She shrugged. 'Ironically, I had been planning to leave him once the girls were both settled at uni. But then Mum was ill with dementia.' She grimaced. 'I'm not proud of myself for manipulating Steve, but he'd just come out of an affair, and he was always a bit more likely to agree to things when he was feeling guilty. I told him I wanted to take a sabbatical and move Mum in with us for a few months, to look after her for as long as I could. The girls wanted her to be with us, too. But then Mum started calling him by my dad's name, and Steve got really upset about it. He couldn't see that she was confused and didn't mean to call him by the wrong name.'

'It sounds as if you married a man like your dad, and maybe when your mum was ill, she could see that,' Tim said carefully.

'And maybe he realised it, too. He definitely resented the time I spent with Mum, thinking I should've been focusing on him. Eventually he gave me an ultimatum: either I had to put Mum in a home, or he'd leave, because what we had wasn't a marriage any more.'

Tim winced. 'I know I shouldn't judge, but that's *incredibly* mean-spirited. Your mum was ill and you wanted to support her and spend time with her.'

She nodded. 'I called his bluff. And he left.' She looked away. 'It turned out he was seeing someone else. I'd just been so busy with Mum that this time I'd missed the signs. It was before the no-fault divorce rules came in, or I would have agreed to that. But Steve decided to sue me for divorce on the grounds of unreasonable behaviour.'

The more Tim heard, the more he disliked Rachel's ex. How could anyone be that self-centred?

'Unfortunately for him, my solicitor was very good, and Steve discovered that the courts didn't see things in quite the same way that he did. Adultery, on the other hand, did count as unreasonable behaviour—on his part. It got a bit acrimonious, though we're just about civil now, for the girls' sake. And because, once probate from Mum's flat had been agreed, I bought him out of our house.' She looked bleak. 'Actually, I did move my mum into a nursing home, towards the end, and I felt so guilty about it. But Mum needed more care than I could give her, and I wanted her to be comfortable. I visited her every single day. The staff were brilliant—when I came into the reception area, they used to tell me what kind of night she'd had and what sort of mood she was in, and whether she'd taken part in activities. They were so upset when she died. A dozen of them came to her funeral.'

Tim reached across the table to squeeze her hand. 'I'm sorry about your mum. And I'm sorry your ex didn't support you through her last illness. No wonder you're wary of starting another relationship. It must be so hard to trust again when someone's treated you like that.'

'Yes—and that's trusting my own judgement as well as trusting someone else,' she said. 'But it's been hard for you, too. You were happy with Mandy until she died, and you never expected your life to change so suddenly.' She looked at him, her grey eyes wide with sincerity. 'I hope you know I'm not trying to step into her place in your life.'

'I do,' he said. 'It's different—and it's kind of weird, dating again after all these years with one person. I've no idea what the dating rules are nowadays.'

'Neither have I,' she said. 'So let's make a pact. We'll just be ourselves and not what we think each other wants us to be.'

'That works for me,' he said, and chinked his empty coffee mug against hers. 'Here's to getting to know each other and being honest with each other.'

'Getting to know each other and being honest with each other,' she echoed. 'And ourselves.' She glanced at her watch. 'I really ought to be going.'

'I'll see you home,' he said immediately.

She shook her head. 'You don't have to do that. I'll be fine.'

'At least let me walk you to the station,' he said. 'I know you're perfectly capable of looking after yourself; but, apart from the fact that it's the way my parents brought me up, there's a very selfish bit of me that means I don't quite want to let you go.'

To his relief, she agreed; and he walked hand in hand with her to the station.

'Thank you for this evening. I really enjoyed it,' he said.

'Me, too. And thank you for the coffee.'

He kissed her lightly. 'My pleasure. See you tomorrow.'

And he was smiling all the way home. It was still early days between them but letting her a tiny bit more into his life felt good. Maybe, just maybe, she was the one who'd help him move on from the yawning ache of loss—just as he might be the one who could help her move on after an unhappy marriage to a truly selfish man.

CHAPTER FIVE

'PETER BELLINGHAM, AGED FIFTY-SIX,' Lorraine the triage nurse said. 'He had chest pains, and I've run an ECG but it's clear. He's got a headache and a temperature, he's been feeling unwell for about four days, and he looks as if he's got mumps. He didn't want to come in and he's convinced it's all a fuss about nothing, but his wife insisted on bringing him in.'

'Thanks, Lorraine,' Rachel said, and introduced herself to the patient and his wife when they came through.

'I don't know why we're here. It's just a bug,' Peter Bellingham protested. 'The nurse said my ECG was fine and it's not my heart.'

'But you've got a headache and a temperature, you've had chest pains, and there's the swelling in your neck,' Rachel said. Bilateral, she noticed, around his jaw and lower neck. 'What do you do, Mr Bellingham?'

'I'm a plumber,' he said.

'So if someone's got a dripping tap, or their sink is a bit slow in emptying, would you advise them to sort it out quickly or just leave it until, say, they have their yearly boiler service?'

'Get someone out,' he said, 'because if you leave that sink it'll end up being blocked and it'll be a lot more hassle and cost more to sort out.'

'That's precisely why you're here,' Rachel said with a smile. 'Because if you leave it, you could end up with complications. Would you mind if we examined you?'

'It's just a bug,' he insisted. But then he sighed. 'All right. Go ahead, because it'll stop Sheena worrying when she really doesn't need to.'

She checked his lymph glands and looked in his mouth. His tongue was swollen, as were the tissues under his tongue. She noticed that his submandibular area was tense; it could be a dental abscess, which in turn was causing something more serious. 'Mr Bellingham, have you had any pain in your teeth?' she asked.

'No. Just my neck.'

'I think you might have something called Ludwig's angina,' she said, 'but I want to put a camera down your nose to look at the top part of your airway.'

He frowned. 'Angina? Isn't that to do with my heart? I think one of my uncles had angina—isn't that right, Sheena?'

'I think so,' his wife said.

'Ludwig's angina isn't to do with your heart. It's a type of cellulitis—a bacterial infection involving the inner layers of your skin,' Rachel explains. 'It causes swelling in your neck, which you've already noticed, and swelling in the floor of your mouth.' And it was time-critical, because when the tongue started swelling it could become difficult to stop the airway being compromised. 'I'm going to put a spray up your nose, so it won't be so uncomfortable when I put the tube with the camera in. Are you OK with that?'

He looked fed-up but agreed.

Rachel went to fetch the camera, and bumped into Tim.

'Camera?' he asked, glancing at the instrument in her hand.

'I've got a patient that I think has Ludwig's angina,' she said.

'That's rare. Dental abscess?'

'I think so,' she said. 'But obviously I need to check. If he'd left it much longer, I might've had to give him a tracheotomy to preserve his airway. I still might.'

'Along with the possibility of sepsis and complications,' he said. 'Give me a yell if you need an extra pair of eyes, but your treatment plan sounds the same as mine would be.'

'Cheers,' she said, buoyed by his support.

The camera gave her a good view of her patient's vocal cords, and the swelling was obvious. 'Mr Bellingham, I'm going to send you for a CT scan to see if any pus needs draining—but I think you have an abscess under your tooth, and it's given you a bacterial infection which is causing the pain, the lump in your neck, and the fact you're finding it harder to swallow. The maxillofacial surgeons will have to remove that abscess for you, under a general anaesthetic, and we'll give you antibiotics to sort out the infection. You'll need help breathing until it's all settled down, so we'll need to admit you. And you're lucky you didn't delay it much longer, because it can lead to sepsis—which can be fatal.'

'I could've died?' He looked shocked. 'I thought my wife was just making a fuss.'

'No. You made a good call,' Rachel told his relieved-looking wife.

He shook his head. 'And I don't understand how it can be a tooth abscess when my mouth doesn't hurt.'

'Not all abscesses hurt,' Rachel explained. 'But I'm glad you got it checked out. If you'd left it longer and your throat had started swelling, we might've had to give you a tracheotomy.'

'What, where you have to put a hole in my throat?' He looked shocked.

'In other words, stop being a stubborn middle-aged man,' Sheena Bellingham said, her teasing belied by the worried look in her eyes.

'You did the right thing, making him come in,' Rachel reassured her.

Once Mr Bellingham had the CT scan and Rachel had called down the maxillofacial surgeons, he was taken off to Theatre.

She saw Tim briefly in the staff kitchen during her break and filled him in on her patient's progress.

'That's good to hear. Now, I'll keep this really quick, because it isn't work,' Tim said, clearly mindful that someone else from the team could come into the kitchen at any minute. 'When are you off duty next?'

'Wednesday,' she said.

'Perfect. If the weather's reasonable, do you fancy a day at the beach?'

'That'd be great,' she said. 'Actually, I prefer the beach in autumn and winter.'

'Me, too. I'll call you tonight after work,' he said, 'and we can decide where to go.' He gave her one of those gorgeous smiles that reached his eyes and made her stomach flip, then headed out of the staff room to his office.

True to his word, he video called her later that evening. 'I've been looking at our options. If we go by train, we can reach Brighton in an hour. So we can have an ice cream on the pier; perhaps a look round the Pavilion, if we can get tickets; and a wander through The Lanes, mooching about in the art galleries and antique shops,' he said. 'Or we can get to Rye in about the same amount of time, catch a bus and find ourselves a nice sandy beach to walk along, then go back and explore the town.'

'That's pretty hard to choose,' she said. 'How about we do one this month and one next month?'

'Great idea,' he said, and took a coin from his pocket. 'You call.'

'Heads Rye, tails Brighton,' she said.

He tossed the coin and checked it. 'Heads,' he said, showing her the coin lying on the back of his hand. 'Rye it is.'

'I can't remember the last time I went to Rye. I was probably quite young,' she said.

'It'll be fun,' he promised.

They caught the train from St Pancras on Wednesday morning, then the bus from Rye station to the beach. The weather was perfect; the sun turned the sandy beach to gold, and the sea was a beautiful bright blue. Rachel enjoyed walking hand in hand along the beach with Tim, hearing the swish of the sea as the waves rolled lazily onto the shore and hissed back again. The wind whipped by them, making the top layer of sand spin across the beach; she kissed him, tasting the salty air on his lips. 'This was a great idea of yours,' she said. 'Just us and the sand and the waves.'

When they'd finished their walk and Rachel had taken a couple of snaps of them to-gether, they caught the bus back into town and wandered through the charming cob-bled streets, enjoying the view of the hig-gledy-piggledy half-timbered houses with their mullioned windows. They stopped in a charming ancient pub with heavily beamed ceilings and found a table by the inglenook fireplace with its roaring fire.

'According to the website,' Tim said, 'this place used to be home to smugglers.'

'So those cutlasses on the walls might've once belonged to a pirate,' she said.

'And it's haunted,' Tim said. 'There's a priest's hole in the chimney breast, and that door behind me led to what were once se-cret tunnels.' He smiled. '"Watch the wall, my darling."'

'You've lost me,' Rachel said.

'It's a poem about smugglers. I can't re-member who wrote it, but Hannah did it with her Year Sevens and I remember her doing the lesson prep for it round our kitchen table with Mandy.' He laughed. 'They did the en-tire thing in pirate speak. And I think Han-nah borrowed a pirate hat and eyepatch to teach it.'

'Arr, that be a great idea,' Rachel said, in her best pirate voice, and he groaned.

After lunch, they explored the narrow streets a bit more before taking the train back to London.

'We ought to make a list of places we want to see,' Tim said. 'And things we'd like to do.'

'Hampstead Pergola,' she said. 'And that's open all year round. So we could go later in the winter if it's snowing, or wait for the wisteria in the spring, or just go and see the autumn leaves everywhere right now.'

'All three work for me.' He took his phone out. 'And I've always wanted to do one of those tours when you get to see the Tube stations that aren't open to the public any more. Like going back in time.'

'I'd like that, too. And Hampton Court. For the maze,' she said.

'We could go by river. It'd be fun.'

Between them, and with the help of a couple of websites, they came up with a list of museums, parks, stately homes and unusual buildings they wanted to visit by the time the train pulled into London.

'Thank you,' Tim said when he saw her home. 'I've really enjoyed today. And making our list. It's been a while since I let the world in. You've given me a new perspective.'

'You've done the same for me,' she said. 'Right now is the most fun I've had in a long time.'

He kissed her lingeringly. 'Me, too. I'll see you tomorrow at work.'

On Friday the following week, they spent the morning wandering round the museum at the Royal College of Physicians, fascinated by the seventeenth-century surgical instruments and the collection of everything from bezoar stones to leech jars, and then Tim glanced at his watch. 'Righty. Time for lunch.'

'Are we going to the museum café?' Rachel asked.

'No. I have a table booked somewhere I think you'll really like. And it's a nice day, so it's a pretty walk.'

They headed towards King's Cross and the Regent's Canal; the trees with their remaining few leaves were reflected perfectly in the water, looking incredibly pretty.

'So where are we heading? Islington?' she asked.

'Not quite,' he said.

A few minutes later, he stopped beside a narrowboat with 'The Cheese Barge' painted along its side. 'We're having afternoon tea for lunch,' he said. 'Except there's no cake.'

'Afternoon cheese,' she said with a smile. 'Sounds perfect.'

And it was: finger sandwiches, a mini cheese toastie and a mini English muffin topped with Welsh Rarebit, two warm cheese scones, and then a range of cheeses paired with very posh crackers, celery and grapes.

'And there's a pink sugar mouse,' she said, delighted. 'Tim, this is genius.'

'Isn't it just?'

After lunch, they walked along the canal to the Angel and caught the Tube back to Hampstead. They were curled up together on her sofa, kissing, when the front door banged.

'Mum, we're home! Surprise!' Meg and Saskia came into the living room, still wearing their coats because they were clearly too eager to see her to take them off and hang them up first; and then, seeing her move away from Tim on the sofa, they stopped dead. 'Oh.'

Busted, Rachel thought. Very busted. She

hadn't been ready to tell her daughters about Tim, yet, but it looked as if she was going to have to explain. 'Let me introduce you,' she said. 'Meg, Saskia, this is Tim. My boss.'

He coughed. 'That's merely in admin terms. We work as a team in my department.'

'*Your* department,' Rachel teased.

Meg and Saskia looked at Tim, at how close he was sitting to their mother, and then at each other. Rachel could feel colour rising in her face. No doubt her mouth was slightly reddened and swollen, too. Ridiculously, it felt as if she and Tim were the teenagers and her mum had come in unexpectedly to find them kissing on the sofa, rather than her being the mum and her adult children being the ones walking in.

'It's nice to meet you, Tim,' Meg said politely, and held her hand out to shake his.

'Very nice,' Saskia added, shaking his hand in turn. 'It's about time Mum had something lovely going on in her life.' She gave Rachel a pointed look. 'Don't try to tell us you're just good friends, either.'

Yeah. She'd known that one wouldn't work.

'Do you mind?' Tim asked.

'No. Provided you don't behave like our dad did,' Saskia said bluntly.

'No. That's not who I am. And, if things work out between your mum and me, I wouldn't try to take his place,' he reassured them. 'Since you've both had a long train journey—Manchester and Sheffield, if I remember rightly—you must be in severe need of a mug of tea. Sit down with your mum and I'll go and put the kettle on. Milk? Sugar? And would you prefer tea or coffee?'

They smiled approvingly at him. 'Thank you. That's so kind. Coffee for me, please— just milk,' Meg said.

'Me, too, please,' Saskia said. 'Except—'

'You're vegan, so you need non-dairy milk,' he said. 'That's in the cupboard underneath the kettle, right?' he asked Rachel.

'Yes, it is,' she said, grateful for both his tact at giving her some time alone with her daughters, and the kindness of making them a hot drink after their journeys.

Meg and Saskia took off their coats and placed them on the back of an armchair; the second Tim had left the room, they pounced. 'You kept him quiet, Mum,' Meg said.

Rachel winced. 'It's early days. *Very* early days.'

'Do you like him?' Saskia asked.

'Yes,' Rachel confirmed.

'Then that's all right,' Meg said. 'Because he seems to like you, too.'

'I can't believe he knew about me having non-dairy milk,' Saskia said. 'Dad never remembers, and I've been vegan for two and a half years.'

'Tim's one of the good guys,' Rachel said softly. 'He notices the little things.' Though she couldn't say it was because of his job, because Steve would've needed to pay just as much attention to detail in his own job. The difference was, Tim didn't put himself first, second and third. Not that she wanted to point out Steve's faults in front of his daughters; she wanted to try and keep that relationship as uncomplicated and smooth as possible. 'So you're both home for the weekend?'

'Yes. I know we should've checked you were off duty, first, but we just wanted to see you,' Meg said.

She hugged them both in turn. 'You never, *ever* have to ask to come home. You live here. And I've really missed you both.'

They hugged her back even harder. 'Love you, Mum,' Saskia said.

Tim came back in with tray of coffee and biscuits for all of them, then sat chatting to Meg and Saskia about their courses, and Meg's plans for teaching. Somehow, it felt natural for him to stay for dinner; Tim confessed he was hopeless in the kitchen but insisted on doing the washing up. And when Meg got out her guitar after dinner, they all ended up singing along, something Rachel knew Meg had always wished her dad would do with them, but Steve had never quite had the patience.

When Tim had left, Meg said, 'I really like him, Mum. I think he'll be good for you.'

'We might be good for each other,' Rachel said, 'but, as I said earlier, we haven't been together long and we're keeping it low profile. I don't want to rush into things. As far as everyone at work is concerned, we're just good friends.'

'Does Jenny know you're seeing him?' Saskia asked.

Rachel laughed. 'Yes. According to her I was glowing after our dance aerobics class last week, and it wasn't just because I'd put in extra effort that evening. She made me tell her everything. We met her for a drink, and she likes him.'

'Obviously he works with you, so that's how you met him. Is he divorced, too?' Meg asked.

'Widowed,' Rachel explained. 'There was a tragic accident, a couple of years ago. His wife was allergic to sesame. She went out to dinner with friends, and her food was accidentally cooked in sesame oil; she collapsed and hit her head in the wrong place.'

Saskia winced. 'How awful. Poor woman. And poor Tim.' She paused. 'Does he have kids?'

'Two girls, a bit older than you,' Rachel said. 'Hannah, the elder one, is an English teacher and is expecting her first baby in a few weeks, and Sophie has a marketing consultancy.'

'What are they like?' Meg asked.

'I haven't met them yet,' Rachel said.

'You're so lovely that they're bound to like you straight away,' Saskia said.

'Or see me as someone trying to step into their mum's shoes,' Rachel said quietly.

Meg shook her head. 'Even if they worry about you doing that, they'll know as soon as they meet you. That isn't who you are—unlike *some* people we could mention.'

Rachel sighed, knowing they meant the way their dad had foisted various girlfriends on them; he'd split up from the woman he'd left her for and moved on several more times since. 'I don't want you to fall out with your dad. He does love you, you know.'

'Mum, let's be honest about it. The person Dad loves most is himself,' Saskia said. 'He's never been in the running for Dad of the Year. We've learned not to expect anything from him, and that means we never feel let down. On the rare occasions he does actually do something thoughtful, then it's a bonus.'

'I'm sorry,' Rachel said. It was easy to see things in hindsight, but maybe she'd been wrong to stay with him and put up with his behaviour for all those years. Maybe she should have asked him to leave when the girls were small. Being a single parent had been a struggle for her own mother, but perhaps it would have been better for her daughters if Rachel had been a single parent. She'd never discussed it with them, not wanting to make their relationship with their father even rockier; but she had a nasty feel-

ing that, despite the way she'd tried to protect them from knowing about their dad's
affairs, they'd picked up on it anyway.

'It's not your fault, Mum,' Meg said.

'Anyway. Let's talk about something else.
Are you off at any point, this weekend, and
can we do something?' Saskia asked.

'I'm off tomorrow,' Rachel said, 'and I'm
working a late on Sunday. So I'm all yours
tomorrow and Sunday morning.'

Meg flicked into the internet. 'It's another
fortnight until the rink's open at Somerset
House, or I'd suggest ice skating and hot
chocolate.'

'I know we've got our own personal emergency doctor, but do you really want to risk
falling over and hurting your wrist or your
hands so you can't practise a piece, when
you've got Finals this year?' Saskia asked.

'Good point,' Meg said. 'We'll have to
think of something else.'

'How about the Natural History Museum,
followed by cake somewhere nice, then back
home to watch *Mamma Mia*?' Saskia suggested. 'We haven't done any of that for
ages.'

'Fine by me. Mum?' Meg asked.

Rachel nodded. 'We can order a takeaway

tomorrow night. There's a new Thai place that's just opened round the corner, and apparently, they have really good vegan and veggie options. I was waiting until you were home to try it out.'

'That,' Saskia said, giving her a hug, 'sounds perfect.'

Rachel thoroughly enjoyed having the girls home; they reminisced their way through the Natural History Museum, found a gorgeous indie patisserie for cake, sang their way through *Mamma Mia* and discovered that the new takeaway lived up to its reputation. They went for a walk on Hampstead Heath on Sunday morning and had a leisurely brunch at a café before the girls waved her off to work and promised to text her to let her know they were back safely at their respective flats.

She didn't see Tim until after their shift on Monday, when they'd arranged to go for a drink.

'I liked your daughters very much,' he said. 'They're very like you.'

She smiled. 'Thank you.'

'And, considering I've met your girls... I was wondering if you'd like to meet mine. I've told them about you, and they've suggested having dinner at my place.'

'You're cooking?' she asked warily, remembering that he'd said how awful his cooking was.

'Um, no,' he said, 'nothing so dangerous. Hannah's going to make a lasagne, I'm buying the salad and garlic bread, and Sophie's going to make tiramisu. Is there anything there you can't eat?'

'No—it all sounds lovely,' she said.

Though she felt a bit daunted on the Wednesday night as she walked to Tim's house from the Tube station, carrying wine and chocolates. Were his daughters going to feel that she was trying to take over from their mum? And was this too soon in any case? Was she rushing into something that would end up making her feel even lonelier than she'd been before she'd started her new job?

But Hannah and Sophie were warm and welcoming, as were their partners, and made sure she was part of the conversation. Rachel thoroughly enjoyed dinner and insisted on helping to clear the table afterwards. 'As a guest, I really hate being waited on hand and foot. I'd much rather muck in and help, so everything's done more quickly and nobody's left stuck on kitchen duty.'

Tim shooed her back out of the kitchen. 'I'm stacking the dishwasher while the coffee's brewing. Honestly, there's almost nothing to do.'

'Thank you for inviting me tonight,' she said to Hannah and Sophie when she went back to the table with them.

'My pleasure,' Hannah said. 'This is my first official week on maternity leave, and making lasagne gave me something to do, seeing as *someone* banned me from decorating the nursery.' She gave her husband a mock glare.

Rachel smiled. 'I remember being yelled at for using a chair as a stepladder so I could put curtains up in the nursery.'

'Don't give her ideas,' Jamal groaned.

'I'll try not to,' Rachel promised. 'I just wanted you both to know that this thing between your dad and me is very new, and I'm absolutely not trying to step into your mum's shoes, even if things develop between us. I lost my mum earlier this year and I miss her very much, so I have an idea how you must feel.'

'Thank you,' Hannah said.

'Can we be honest with you?' Sophie asked. At Rachel's nod, she continued, 'We worry about Dad being lonely. He has a habit of cocooning himself in work when he doesn't want to talk about things. Since Mum died, he's even kept us at a bit of a distance. But he's loosened up over the last few weeks, so I'm guessing that's your influence.'

'Maybe,' Rachel said. 'My daughters worry about me being lonely, too. And they liked your dad very much when they met him.'

'Dad's pretty awesome,' Hannah said.

Rachel smiled. 'Yes, he is. He's a great doctor—and he's a really nice man.'

'How do you feel about board games?' Sophie asked, eyeing the bare table speculatively.

'Love them,' Rachel said.

They ended up playing Trivial Pursuit. 'Women versus men, I think,' Hannah said.

'I'm hopeless at the sport questions,' Rachel said, 'so I hope you're good.'

'Better than Dad is,' Sophie said, laughing. 'Give him a football question, and nine times out of ten he'll get it wrong.'

'Bring it on, because we're so going to win—right, Jamal and Calum?' Tim asked, blowing on his fingertips and polishing his nails on his sweater.

'If you lose,' Sophie said, 'you're buying us chocolate, Dad. A bar each. A *big* bar.'

'You're the one who's going to be buying chocolate, sweetheart,' he teased back.

It turned out to be a noisy game, with many accusations of the other team having super-easy questions and a lot of laughter. Rachel enjoyed it thoroughly and was shocked to realise how late it was when they'd finished their second game.

'I'd better head for home,' she said, 'because I'm on an early shift tomorrow and my boss is a bit grumpy.'

'Very grumpy, because he's buying all the chocolate,' Sophie crowed. She and Hannah high-fived Rachel then gave her a hug.

'It was really nice to meet you,' Rachel said.

'It was really lovely to meet you, too,' Sophie said. 'We'll have to do this again.'

'Maybe we could have dinner at my place, next time,' Rachel offered. 'I enjoy cooking. Just let me know of any dietary requirements.'

Before they left that evening, Hannah said, 'Rachel's lovely, Dad. I think Mum would've approved of her. She was very careful to let us know she isn't trying to insert herself in Mum's place.'

'Nobody will ever take your mum's place,' Tim said. 'This is something new.'

'And we're glad,' Sophie said. 'We think she'll be good for you.'

Tim thought that Rachel would be good for him, too. Particularly as his daughters liked her.

But.

There was a niggle that wouldn't go away, no matter how hard he tried to ignore it or squash it.

Being a workaholic meant he hadn't been there for his wife when she'd needed him. Would it be the same with Rachel—even though they did the same job, and he was pretty sure she'd understand where he was coming from? Would this all just crash and burn?

Given how unhappy her marriage had obviously been, he didn't want to hurt her. So he was going to have to be really careful. No matter how attractive he found her, they needed to take it slowly. Sensibly.

CHAPTER SIX

'HANNAH AND SOPHIE really liked you,' Tim said when he managed to snatch a coffee break at the same time as Rachel, the next day.

'It's mutual,' she said. 'They're lovely. And that tells me what a gorgeous woman Mandy was, too.'

Then Ediye came into the rest room. 'I know you're both on a break,' she said, 'but I'm in over my head. I have a patient with suspected sepsis.'

Tim and Rachel exchanged a glance. Sepsis was potentially serious, but both of them thought that Ediye was experienced enough to handle the situation.

'And she has motor neurone disease,' she said.

Motor neurone disease was a disorder that affected the nerves controlling the muscles, and eventually made the muscles weaken and waste; it could affect movement, speech and breathing. Although there was no cure, the symptoms could be treated. But MND meant they'd need to take a lot more into account where sepsis was concerned.

'I'll come now,' Rachel said. 'Catch you later, Tim.'

Ediye introduced her to Ginny Morton, their patient, and her partner Bella.

'Ginny was a pharmacology lecturer,' Bella said. 'MND hasn't taken away her intellect, but she can't speak any more. She communicates with her eyes—one blink for yes, two for no.' She wrinkled her nose. 'We do use an alphabet chart, but it's slow and frustrating when you blink to spell a word.'

'I can imagine,' Rachel said. 'Ginny, I'm sorry that I need to ask Bella to answer for you, but Ediye tells me you might have sepsis so, with your background, you'll know why I want to assess you as fast as possible. Can I check you're OK with that?'

Ginny gave a single blink, and Rachel squeezed her hand. 'Thank you. And you're happy for me to examine you?'

Another single blink.

'Thank you. Are you in any pain?'

Two slow blinks. 'That's good,' Rachel said.

The breathing difficulty was apparent; when Rachel listened to Ginny's chest there was little air going in. Given the motor neurone disease, Ginny's ventilation muscles were probably impaired. Her heart rate was faster than Rachel was happy with, and her blood pressure was on the low side; the signs were all pointing towards a severe infection.

'So when did the breathing difficulty start?' she asked.

'Today,' Bella said. 'She was tired, yesterday; this morning, her breathing was bad, and her temperature was up. That's why I called the ambulance.'

'You did the right thing. Ginny, I'm going to send you for a chest X-ray,' Rachel said, 'because I'm not happy about what I'm hearing through the stethoscope. I think it's likely to be an infection, and I'm going to give you some broad-spectrum antibiotics, as well as some fluids and medication to get your blood pressure up. And I want to admit you for monitoring.' She looked at Bella. 'The antibiotics should kick in fairly quickly, but I'm worried about Ginny's breathing.

I'd like her in so we can react quickly if her breathing gets worse. But I'm pretty sure we can get her through this and back home.'

'Good. Because I'm not ready to...' Bella's voice wobbled.

Guessing what the other woman wasn't saying—that she wasn't ready to say good-bye to the woman she loved—Rachel gave her a swift hug. 'Hang on in there,' she said. And she was really glad that she, rather than Tim, had helped Ediye with this case. She had a feeling it would've brought back too many memories for Tim, opening up his scars from losing Mandy.

At the end of November, it was the department's Christmas meal. A couple of evenings beforehand, Tim was curled up with Rachel on her sofa. 'Is it bad to admit that I'm dreading the Christmas meal?' he asked.

Rachel frowned. 'Why are you dreading it? From what I've heard, it's the highlight of the department at Christmas, and everyone loves you doling out the Secret Santa presents.'

'But it's the start of Christmas.' Tim wrinkled his nose. 'And you know what Christmas is like in the department. All the winter ailments, the fractures from icy days, and then Christmas itself when people start drinking and falling out, and we have to spend half our time patching them up.'

'Yes, but that's only some of the population,' she reminded him. 'Most people enjoy the chance to spend time with the people they love, eating too much and playing board games and...' She looked at him. 'What's this really about, Tim?'

He shook his head, not wanting to put it into words. 'Nothing.'

She folded her arms and stared at him, waiting.

He sighed and gave in. 'OK. Mandy really, really loved Christmas. She always made a big thing of it—the decorations, the music, the food, the Christmas get-togethers. I've had two Christmases where I just haven't been able to face her not being there on Christmas Day, and I've worked late so I don't have time to think. I've been a coward and made my girls go to their in-laws for Christmas Day, because I know I can't make them the sort of Christmas their mum did.' He grimaced. 'And it worries me that they might think I'm pushing them away.'

'I'm sure they understand,' Rachel said.

Something in her expression made him wonder if they'd confided in her. He sighed. 'I know I could order Christmas and get it delivered in a box, but that'd feel wrong, too, because it isn't what the day's meant to be about. And it feels wrong to celebrate Christmas in our house, when Mandy was the centre of it.'

'I think,' she said, 'you're panicking. And it sounds to me as if you're trying too hard.'

'How?'

'This is going to sound harsh, but you need to accept that you just can't have Christmas like you did with Mandy, not any more. It's always going to be different now,' she said.

And that was what he couldn't handle.

'But different doesn't mean that you're pushing her out of your life or pretending that she never existed,' she said, reaching out to hold both his hands. 'If you start accepting that things will change from year to year, it means you can cherish your memories of the good times instead of focusing on what you've lost. The last Christmas you had with Mandy was very different from your first Christmas together, yes?'

'Yes,' he agreed. 'That last Christmas,

it was dinner for sixteen because everyone came to us. A roast turkey, veggie options, all the trimmings, three puddings, crackers and charades and board games. But our first Christmas—we spent it in a pokey little flat, where we barely had the space to put up a tiny artificial Christmas tree. I was working an early shift, and Mandy was determined to cook Christmas dinner for us and our parents because it was our first Christmas together. We didn't have space for a dining table, so everyone was going to eat off trays. She'd got everything planned and this mammoth timetable. Except the oven went wrong, so she couldn't even cook the pigs in blankets, let alone the turkey.' He smiled, remembering. 'She probably should've admitted defeat and begged one of the parents to let us cook at their place instead. But Mandy refused to give in and did the lot on the hob. She diced the turkey and made it into a kind of Christmas stew, including the pigs in blankets and stuffing balls. There was a mountain of mashed potato, and the most vile boiled sprouts.' He smiled. 'And it didn't matter.'

'Because you were together. Which is

entirely what Christmas is about,' she said gently.

'On the first of December,' he said, 'she always made Christmas Stew. So we could remember and laugh about it.' He blinked hard. 'The sprouts got better, though.'

She squeezed his hand. 'Mandy sounds like an amazing woman.'

'She was. And I know she'd be furious with me for moping and acting like a wet weekend at her favourite time of year. I know I need to move on. And I want to move on. I really do.'

'You know that with your head,' she said, 'but not with your heart.'

'I don't know how to change that,' he said. He'd been trying. But Christmas felt like an enormous iceberg sliding into his path.

'How about this: even if Mandy had still been here with you, Christmas would've been different this year because you might have a new grandchild to celebrate with,' she said. 'Next year, it will change again, because the baby's going to be old enough to start realising what's going on, and the year after that new traditions might start—Christmas carols and mince pies at nursery, going as a family to take the baby to see

Father Christmas, or maybe everyone spending Christmas at Hannah and Jamal's rather than everyone congregating at yours.'

Tim knew Rachel had a valid point, but he still couldn't make himself feel it.

'You're a Christmas-aholic, aren't you?' he asked.

'I'm afraid so,' she said. 'Last Christmas was awful. Mum was battling pneumonia and she didn't know any of us. Steve had just slapped me with the divorce papers. We were supposed to be going to his family's for Christmas Day because Steve wouldn't be there, but at the last minute he decided to go and take his new girlfriend. Thank God, my sister-in-law warned me he'd changed his plans; I ducked out of going, because I wasn't sure whether he was going to be sniping at me or ostentatiously snogging his girlfriend every two minutes to show me what I was missing.'

Tim felt another surge of dislike towards Rachel's ex. Christmas was a time to try and heal the rifts, not widen them. And didn't the man care about the hurt he was causing his daughters?

'The girls didn't want me to be on my own on Christmas Day, so we stayed at home and had a very non-traditional Christmas dinner. Which was fine. We still managed to find the love. We caught up with Steve's family later, when Steve had gone off skiing. And this year,' she said, 'we're making up for it. We'll be doing all our old traditions, with extra chocolate and gin.'

Making up for what they'd missed. He understood that, but he couldn't find the heart to do it himself. It was just too, too big.

Rachel was clearly trying to help him, so he'd try and meet her halfway. 'What are your family traditions?'

'The girls and I always have a Christmas movie night—when Mum was alive, she joined us, too. We all put on a Christmas jumper, we make big mugs of hot chocolate laced with cream liqueur—a vegan version for Saskia—we start working our way through the Christmas shortbread, and we cuddle up on the sofa under a fleecy throw and watch movies. Usually there's at least *Love Actually* and *Elf.*'

It was just the sort of thing that Mandy had done with their girls.

'We used to go skating at the Natural History Museum or Somerset House, though with Meg being in her Finals year we're giving it a miss this year—the last thing she needs is a sprain or fracture that means she can't practise a piece for her exams. And I always make them stockings.' She grinned. 'I don't care that they're eighteen and twenty-one, and neither do they. They still hang a stocking on their door, and I fill it after they've gone to bed. Lots of little things that I pick up during the year, plus the last-minute stuff that I don't want to be out of date. I normally include a chocolate reindeer and a sugar mouse, a decoration for the Christmas tree, a miniature bottle of flavoured gin, make-up, nail varnish and something ridiculous to make them laugh, like a wind-up toy. I've got personalised plectrums for Meg, this year, and packets of herb seeds for Saskia.' She looked wistful. 'I used to make a stocking for Steve, even before we had the girls; I always bought a crazy gadget from the shop at the Science Museum for his desk, a miniature bottle of brandy, and Christmas-themed chocolate.'

Tim noticed what was missing. What went in Rachel's stocking? 'What about you? Didn't you get a stocking?'

'Once the girls were old enough to stop believing in Santa, they collaborated with

Mum,' Rachel said. 'Even last year, when Mum could barely string a sentence together, they made time to sit with her and chat about Christmases past. I have no idea how they managed to help her write a Christmas card to me—it must've been before the pneumonia really knocked her for six—but that's the most precious gift I could've had. The last Christmas card, in her own handwriting.' Tears shimmered in her eyes for a second.

Tim put his arms round her and held her close. 'And this is your first Christmas without her.'

'Yes. She died in January,' she said.

'The first Christmas without them is the roughest one,' he said. 'But your mum will be here with you in spirit. She'll be there in your memories. That'll never go away.'

A single tear spilled over her lashes, and he kissed it away.

'That goes for you, too, you know,' she said shakily.

'Yeah. Mandy always did stockings for our girls, too. I do them, now, because I don't want them to miss out.' It was about the only thing he managed to do for Christmas.

'I bet they really appreciate it,' she said.

He nodded. 'But I don't have Mandy's touch. It feels like going through the motions. They're always nice about it, but I'm sure I've fallen short, and I don't understand where I'm going wrong.'

'Maybe,' she said, 'we can do a joint shopping trip. One just for stocking fillers.'

It filled him with dread and anticipation in equal measures. He had a feeling that Rachel loved Christmas even more than Mandy had; he wasn't sure he could live up to her ideals, and he didn't want to let her down. But, given that this was going to be her first Christmas without her mum, he didn't want to back away from her either.

'I assume you put up a real tree, rather than an artificial one?' he asked.

'Yes, because I love the scent. I always buy it on the first of December. And I've still got the tree decorations that the girls made me at nursery—the yogurt pots painted like a bell with a pipe-cleaner clapper, the salt dough Christmas tree with the splodges of paint for baubles. It doesn't matter that they're getting a bit tatty now, because they were made with love. And I make my own front door wreath.'

Of course she did. Tim felt even more inadequate. He'd avoided any kind of Christmas decorating for the last two years, because it had just been too hard to make the effort. With every stretch, the paper-thin walls around his grief had shredded even further.

'Even last year, I made a wreath for the door,' she said. 'I took all the bits to Mum's room. I chatted to her about the times we'd made wreaths together, I made a playlist of Christmas songs she loved, and I sat there holding her hand and singing until she fell asleep. Then I worked on the wreath until she woke up.' Her smile was bright, though tinged with sadness. 'I'll make a Christmas wreath for her grave, too, this year. An eco one, full of berries to feed the birds. She loved watching the birds in the garden.'

So had Mandy. And there was a huge lump in his throat. Rachel was so brave about this. Why couldn't he be brave, too?

'What are you doing for Christmas, this year?' she asked.

'Working,' he said. 'The girls will go to their in-laws, just like they have for the last two years. It's fine.'

'Do your girls love Christmas?' she asked gently.

He nodded.

'Do you want to be with them?'

'Yes,' he said, 'and no. Yes, because I'm their dad and of course I want to spend family time with them. I love them.'

She waited.

The old doctor's trick, of waiting until your patient told you what was really wrong, worked just as well on someone who wasn't a patient, because he found himself admitting, 'And no, because I feel so inadequate and I can't do things the way their mum did, and I find Christmas just too much.'

'Have you talked to them about it?'

'No. I'm not great at talking about feelings. I never have been.' He glanced at her and could see on her face that she was thinking, *But that's what he's doing right now.* 'It's different with you,' he said. 'I can talk to you.'

'Why?'

'I don't know.' He shook his head. 'I just can.'

'I'm taking that as a compliment,' she said. 'Did you have any traditions that you did with them particularly?'

'Obviously Mandy and I took them to see

Santa when they were tiny, but they're too old for that now.'

'What about going to a carol service, or to one of the Christmas markets, or just out for a walk to see the Christmas lights?' She smiled. 'I would suggest ice skating, but with Hannah being so close to her due date it wouldn't be fair for her to have to sit on the sidelines and watch.'

'I used to take the girls to see the Christmas lights when they were small,' he said, 'and I kind of feel I ought to let the people in the department with small kids have the time to spend with them, because mine are old enough to wait.' He shrugged. 'I know Hannah has a baking session with Sophie for the school Christmas fair. They make gingerbread reindeer and mince pies. But you know how hopeless I am in the kitchen. I'd just get in the way if I tried to help.'

'Maybe you could be their official barista and washer-upper, if you want to join in,' she suggested gently. 'Or maybe you need to make a new tradition, something they didn't do with Mandy. Something to make new memories that will help you smile when you remember the old memories, like your Christmas Stew, instead of wanting to howl inside because you can't do the old stuff any more.'

'I…' He looked helplessly at her. 'I don't know where to start.'

'You could do some things with me, maybe,' she said, 'and if you think it's something the girls might like to do with you then you can suggest doing it with them, too.' She paused. 'I happen to be working on Christmas Day as well. Meg and Saskia are volunteering to serve dinner at a shelter, and we're going to make a proper Christmas dinner for the three of us on Boxing Day. The whole thing—a vegan filo pastry thing for Sophie and turkey for Meg and me, all the trimmings, a fresh pineapple and really good ice cream for pudding. We're going to raise a glass of Prosecco and gin to Mum and eat way too much chocolate.' She looked at him. 'Why don't you all come to us on Boxing Day: you, your girls and their partners? That way, it'll be something new; and because it'll be here, rather than at your place, it means you won't have constant reminders of Mandy not being there.'

He just stared at her, not knowing what to say.

'It's not a way of pushing Mandy away or

pretending she didn't exist,' she reminded him. 'It's helping you come to terms with things so you can remember the good times and smile. So you can enjoy Christmas again with your girls—all the important family stuff.'

'That's incredibly generous of you,' he said, 'and bits of me really want to say yes. But it's taking up time you'll want to spend with your girls. It's not fair to just expect them to host people they don't know.'

'I'm pretty sure they'll say yes,' she said.

So was he, because he'd met them and he'd had the distinct impression that they'd both inherited their mum's huge heart. But he wasn't taking any of it for granted. 'Ask them first,' he said.

'All right,' she said, 'and then you ask your girls.'

As Rachel had expected, Meg and Saskia agreed immediately. And Hannah and Sophie were delighted to accept the invitation.

Hannah—after Tim had checked that Rachel wouldn't mind if he gave her number to his daughters—called her. 'It's really kind of you to ask us, Rachel.'

'It's not kind of me at all. If anything, it's totally selfish,' Rachel said.

'How do you work that out?'

'I miss having a really big family Christmas, because my family now is just my girls,' Rachel explained. 'Even though my ex's family get on with me and still see us, it's a bit too awkward still for me to accept an invite to a family thing if my ex is going to be there.'

'It's going to be really good spending the time with Dad, but he hates Christmas because...' Hannah stopped. 'Sorry.'

'Because your mum loved Christmas and he can't cope with it without her. I know, love,' Rachel said gently. 'Probably because I never knew your mum, he's able to talk about her to me and be honest about how he feels. I'm hoping I can make him see Christmas a bit differently this year. I'm not pushing your mum out at all—I know I've already told you that, but I really want to make sure you and Sophie don't feel I'm intruding. I'm simply hoping that he can make some new memories that will help him remember how to enjoy the old ones and also keep him close to you.'

'That,' Hannah said, 'would be amazing—and it means this'll be the first good Christmas we've had in three years. But it's also not fair to expect you to do everything. What can we do to help?'

'How about,' Rachel suggested, 'you bring pudding? Maybe Sophie can make her amazing tiramisu or something. But honestly, the best thing you can bring is yourselves and a smile. Oh, and let me know of any—' she balked at the word 'allergy', not wanting to trample on a sore spot '—dietary requirements. There's going to be a vegan option, because of Saskia. It's a filo pastry snake filled with veggies, pearl barley, apricots and spices, and she's making a spicy tomato sauce to go with it.'

'That sounds good.' Hannah chuckled. 'Dad tells me you're as much of a cheese fiend as he is. So we'll bring cheese, too. And a vegan one for Saskia.'

'Perfect,' Rachel said, 'and I'll make cheese biscuits.'

'The ones you took into the department and Dad raved about? That sounds wonderful.'

'We have board games,' Rachel said, 'and including one where you have to play kazoos and guess the song. Meg usually plays the piano so we can sing our heads off. And there will be chocolate.'

'I can't wait,' Hannah said.

It was the first time in three years that Tim had actually enjoyed the team Christmas meal out, and it was all thanks to Rachel. They were still keeping their relationship quiet at work, but he couldn't help glancing at her when he donned a Santa hat to hand out the Secret Santa presents. And, even though she was sitting at the other end of the table from him, she met his gaze every so often and gave him an encouraging smile. He danced with everyone in the team after the meal; his dance with Rachel wasn't the slow one he longed for, though he consoled himself that at least it helped him keep up the pretence at work that they were just good friends because it meant he wouldn't slip up and accidentally kiss her in front of the department.

Because they lived in different parts of the city, they left the party separately; but Tim had arranged beforehand to catch a taxi from his place to Rachel's. When she opened the front door to him, he smiled.

'You look absolutely gorgeous in that dress, Ms Halliday.'

'You scrub up rather nicely yourself, Mr Hughes,' she teased back. 'Can I tempt you to a glass of wine?'

'Yes, please.' He handed her a bottle of chilled pink Prosecco.

'Thank you. Nice choice,' she said. 'Come into the kitchen.' She deftly opened the bottle without spilling a drop, poured them both a glass, and handed one to him. 'So did you enjoy tonight?'

'Yes,' he said, 'thanks to you. But I wish I'd had a chance to dance with you a bit more.'

'That can be arranged,' she said, putting her glass on the worktop and picking up her phone. 'Christmas mix?'

'Something slow and bluesy is more what I've got in mind,' he said.

She found a playlist on her streaming app and connected her phone to the speaker. 'Like this?'

'Perfect,' he said, as Fleetwood Mac's 'Need Your Love So Bad' came on. He put his own glass down, hung his jacket over the back of a chair and drew her into his arms. 'This is what I wanted to do earlier,' he said, 'but not in front of everyone. I don't want to make things awkward for us at work.'

'I know. It's sensible,' she said. 'Though at the same time it makes me feel a bit like a dirty little secret.'

'You're not a dirty little secret. Not at all,' he said. 'It just saves the complications, that's all. The people who are important know. The rest can wait until we're ready.'

'I guess.' She rested her head on his shoulder and swayed with him to the music; he closed his eyes, enjoying the feel of her arms wrapped round him and the warmth of her body against his. He wasn't sure which of them moved first, but then he was kissing her, his eyes closed, everything focused on the way her lips moved against his.

He really, *really* liked this woman.

And he wanted more. Except it wasn't fair to rush her. He was meant to be taking this slowly.

Gently, he broke the kiss and dragged himself out of her arms. 'I'd better go before I outstay my welcome.'

She held his gaze, her grey eyes huge. 'Maybe you're not outstaying it.'

His heart rate speeded up a notch when

she added, 'We're both on a late tomorrow, so we don't have to be up early.'

He caught his breath. 'Are you asking...?'

'If you like porridge for breakfast. Oh, and just in case you were wondering, I bought a new bed after I split up with Steve, and I've redecorated the room.'

'There won't be any comparisons,' he said softly. 'For either of us. Though I probably should warn you it's been a while since I've slept with anyone, and decades since I slept with anyone except my wife.'

'Me, too,' she said. 'So maybe we both need to get the awkward stuff over and done with. This isn't going to be perfect. It's going to be different.'

'But it's still you and me,' he said.

'Bring your glass,' she said, scooping up her own glass and the bottle; she took his hand and led him up to her bedroom.

It was a pretty room with a wrought iron bedstead, floral curtains and pale blue walls. She put her glass and the bottle on her bedside table and switched on the lamp; he placed his glass next to hers.

'Are you sure about this?' he asked.

'Bits of me are scared that this is rushing it. But bits of me have wanted this since the first time you kissed me,' she admitted.

He appreciated her honesty. 'I'm not sure if I'm more thrilled or scared.'

'Born again teenagers, the pair of us,' she said.

Slowly, slowly, she removed his tie and undid the buttons of his shirt. Her hands were shaking, he noticed; just as his were when he undid the zip of her dress.

Colour bloomed across her cheeks as she turned to face him. 'I don't have a condom but, just so you know, I haven't slept with anyone in two years and there's absolutely no chance I can get pregnant.'

'I haven't slept with anyone since Mandy died,' he said, wanting to reassure her that she didn't need to worry about STDs; as a doctor, she'd be very aware of their effects. 'And I don't have a condom, either. But if you want to wait, there are other things we can do.'

'So there are,' she said, and her smile made his heart feel as if it had just done a backflip.

She stepped out of her dress and hung it over the top of her cheval mirror; though he noticed how tense her shoulders were.

'The thing about being a born again teenager rather than an original one,' he said, stepping out of his trousers and hanging them on the cheval mirror too, 'is that we do our own laundry and tidy up after ourselves.'

The ridiculous joke made her laugh and took the tension out of her, to his relief. He drew her into his arms and kissed her; when the kiss turned heated, he scooped her up, pushed the duvet aside and laid her against the pillows.

'You're beautiful, Rachel,' he said, 'and you make me feel things I never thought I'd ever feel again.'

'It's the same for me,' she said, stroking his face.

He made love with her, enjoying finding out how and where she liked to be touched, what made her gasp with pleasure; and in turn he enjoyed the way she explored him.

Afterwards, he cradled her in his arms. For the first time in years, the bed didn't feel too wide. It didn't matter that he was lying in a strange bed, because he was getting to know the woman lying in his arms—and it felt as if he was finally coming out of the darkness that had smothered him for the last two years.

* * *

The next morning, Rachel woke, warm and comfortable; then she turned over and realised the bed beside her was empty.

A little flutter of panic went through her as she opened her eyes. Clearly, they'd taken it too fast last night and she shouldn't have asked him to stay. It was obvious that he'd woken before her and had left, feeling embarrassed and ashamed about what they'd done, and too awkward to face her.

But when she sat up, planning to change into her workout gear and run her own shame and embarrassment off before she went to work, she glanced over to the mirror and realised that Tim's trousers and shirt were still there. *He hadn't left.*

A few moments later, she heard footsteps on the stairs, and he appeared in the doorway, wearing just his boxer shorts and carrying two mugs of coffee.

'Good morning,' he said.

She could feel her skin heating. For pity's sake; she was fifty-two, not nineteen. 'Morning,' she mumbled.

He put both mugs of coffee on her side of the bed—he'd obviously taken the bottle and glasses downstairs when he went to make coffee—then bent down to kiss the tip of her nose. 'At our age, the walk of shame is supposed to be when we've forgotten that we're driving and had one glass of wine too many. But I'm dropping thirty years and being the med student who goes home the next morning in his party clothes from the night before.' He climbed back into bed beside her. 'Regretting it?'

'No. And yes,' she admitted. 'I don't regret what we did; but I do feel a bit awkward this morning and I don't really know what to say to you.'

'"Thank you for the coffee, Tim" would do,' he teased.

She smiled. 'Yes. Thank you for the coffee. Maybe I'll have worked out the etiquette for this sort of thing by the time I'm eighty.'

'You'll still be beautiful when you're eighty,' he said. 'That bone structure and those amazing eyes.'

She hadn't expected the compliment and it felt all the sweeter. 'Thank you. You've got gorgeous eyes, too. It was the first thing I noticed about you, when you interviewed me. The colour of cornflowers.' She felt brave enough to trace the line of his jaw and steal a kiss. 'You'll be beautiful at eighty, too.'

'So what happens now?' he asked.

'We could have breakfast together. Here, I mean,' she said. 'And we're on a late. So we don't actually have to have breakfast until late...'

'I like your thinking,' he said, and leaned over to kiss her.

CHAPTER SEVEN

OVER THE NEXT few days, Rachel felt happier than she'd been in years. At work, she and Tim kept things polite and professional with each other, but since that night together things had changed outside work: he was more tactile, easier with her, and she enjoyed the closeness. By unspoken arrangement, he stayed over the nights before they were both on a late shift, and it was so good to wake in his arms and feel that the day would be full of sunshine.

One evening, she took him to the Christmas market on the South Bank as part of the plan to make Christmas less difficult for him. As they walked through the crowds between the wooden chalets, Christmas music was playing, and the air smelled of spice and oranges. There was a nip of frost in the air, and they could see people's breath like mist rising up to the twinkling lights as they chattered and laughed.

She bought them both a hot chocolate, liberally laced with cream liqueur, and they browsed the stalls that sold all kinds of Christmas decorations and gifts, from wooden ornaments and toys to jewellery to candles.

'These stars are gorgeous,' she said. 'I'm definitely buying these for the girls' stockings, this year.'

Tim, too, bought a selection of stocking fillers for his daughters; then they grabbed something to eat from one of the food stalls before walking over Waterloo Bridge and wandering over to watch the skaters at the Somerset House ice rink.

'You know, if we hang around here much longer, we're going to end up working,' Tim said. 'At the very least, there's going to be a Colles' fracture, not to mention sprains, strains and a lot of bruising.'

She tucked her arm through his. 'I know ice skating is maybe not the safest thing, but my girls used to love going here, or to the rink outside the Natural History Museum. It's the combination of the lights, the music, the smell of hot chocolate and the Christmas trees.'

'I have to admit, I'm not really a fan of skating,' he said, 'even if you exclude the Emergency Department aspect of it.'

'I'm not brilliant at actually doing it,' she said, 'but I used to love watching Torvill and Dean. They were so graceful, gliding across the ice and doing those amazing jumps and pirouettes. And I loved her outfits.'

He chuckled. 'You're so showing your age—we must have been students when they won the gold medal.'

'I know.' She laughed back. 'The music I'd choose for ice skating shows my age, too. Robbie Williams...' she sang a snatch of 'She's the One' '...and George Michael.' She grinned. 'And "Last Christmas" is still my favourite contemporary Christmas song ever.'

'Mandy's was Mariah Carey,' he said.

'An excellent choice,' she said. 'I love that one, too. Mandy had good taste.'

'I think,' he said, 'you would've liked each other.'

'I do, too,' she said, and squeezed his hand. 'Have you been to see the Christmas lights at Kew Gardens?'

'No. Mandy went a couple of times with the girls, but I was working.'

'Drop the guilt,' she said, 'and think of the people you helped on those nights. People who were in pain—people who might have died. You made a difference.'

'I guess.' He paused. 'Have you been to Kew?'

'I went with Steve, three or four years back.' She shrugged. 'But it was a work thing, so he spent the whole night networking. I'm planning to go on my own this year and just enjoy the lights and the music and the Christmassy feel.' It was part of her plan to do things for herself again, but maybe it would help Tim, too. 'You're welcome to join me, if you like.'

'Actually, that sounds really nice,' he said. 'And, just to prove I'm serious, I'll book the tickets now.' He grabbed his phone and flicked into the internet. 'Thursday night?'

'Thursday night works for me,' she said.

'This is way better than I remember it,' Rachel said when they were partway through the trail at Kew. 'This is amazing. It must've taken hours to put all those lights over the trees—especially all the way to the top of that beech tree.'

'And those colour-changing butterflies,' he said. 'Though I think my favourites are the ones where the lights look like snow-flakes falling.'

There were little wooden huts on the way, selling Christmassy food and hot spiced cider; and there was a mini fairground in the middle, with old-fashioned rides and Christmassy music played on a steam organ.

'I always loved the gallopers when I was a kid,' Tim said, gesturing to the horses on the carousel.

'Me, too,' Rachel said. 'This will be per-fect for your grandchild in about two years, with the train and the pedal car and the swing boats.'

'And Father Christmas, with real rein-deer,' he said. 'Actually, I think the girls would really like this.'

'Make a date with them,' she said.

'I will,' he agreed. Rachel's delight in Christmas was making it so much more bearable for him, this year. And maybe this would become a new tradition, something to look forward to. With her.

The trail took them over a bridge, where

the reflections of the lights in the water were stunning; through a light arch, which felt like being in a cathedral; and then an area where the lights on the Christmas trees changed in time with the music. Finally there were lasers projected onto water which sprayed across the lake.

'Thank you for coming with me,' he said when they finally left the gardens. 'That was spectacular.'

'Wasn't it? I can't work out what I liked most,' she said. 'I think all of it, actually.'

But it wasn't just the prettiness of the lights and the fabulous presentation, Tim thought. What had made it magical for him was Rachel. Walking hand in hand with her, stealing a kiss, sharing a smile. In the few short weeks he'd known her, she'd chased so many of the shadows away. And he was starting to think that maybe, just maybe, he'd found happiness again.

The following evening, they were both on a late shift when the paramedics brought a little girl into Resus. 'This is Willow Patterson—she's a year old in two days' time,' Samir, the paramedic, said. 'Mrs Patterson, her grandmother, has come in with us, and

Willow's parents are on their way in. She went limp and then started fitting, and her gran called us straight away.'

'Do you know how long the seizure lasted?' Rachel asked.

'Twenty minutes,' Samir said.

Rachel and Tim exchanged a glance. Febrile convulsions were common in that age group, but the fit lasted typically for about five minutes. In this case, it could be encephalitis or epilepsy causing the seizure. And very young children could become extremely unwell very, very quickly.

'In the van, her eyes kept going to the left for about fifteen minutes,' Samir said. 'We've put her on oxygen. Her temperature's a bit higher than normal, but nothing I'd be worried about.'

'OK. Mrs Patterson, we're going to give her some medication to control her seizure, but the medication depresses breathing so we'll need to help her breathe for a little while,' Tim said. 'It's going to look scarier than it is. You're welcome to stay, or if you want to wait outside for her parents to arrive, that's fine.'

'I'll stay,' Mrs Patterson said. 'Can I hold her hand?'

'Yes,' Tim said. 'Rachel, would you mind bagging while I give her the meds?'

'Of course,' Rachel said, sorting out the oxygen mask and bagging. 'Mrs Patterson, do you know if Willow has ever had a fit before?'

'I'm pretty sure she hasn't,' Mrs Patterson said. 'Ellie—my daughter-in-law—would've said.'

'Has she had a high temperature or any other symptoms of a virus over the last couple of days?' Tim asked.

'She felt a bit hot this evening after Ellie gave her her dinner,' Mrs Patterson said. 'She ate just fine—but Ellie thought she was teething. She and Stu were going to call off going out, but I told them I'd give her some teething crystals and she'd be fine with me.' She looked distraught. 'We were just having a cuddle and a story before I put her to bed, but then she went limp and started having a fit. I panicked and called 999.'

'Which was exactly the right thing to do,' Rachel reassured her. 'Her temperature isn't high enough for it to be a febrile convulsion, but about one in twenty people have a one-off fit in their lifetime. This doesn't mean she definitely has epilepsy, though we'll want to keep an eye on her and check her over.'

'Oh, God. If anything happens to her, Stu and Ellie will never forgive me. They haven't been out for months. I sent them out to see a film and have dinner, so they could have some couple time,' Mrs Patterson said.

'It's not your fault,' Rachel reassured her. 'These things happen. Once the medication's taken effect and she's breathing OK on her own, we'll try and wake her up. You can help us with that, if her mum and dad haven't managed to get here by then.'

'She's such a happy little girl. She's just learned to clap and she's so pleased with herself, doing "If you're happy and you know it",' Mrs Patterson said, looking anxious. 'It's not going to change her, is it?'

'We'll know more when she's awake,' Tim said. 'I remember my girls loved clapping songs.'

'So did mine,' Rachel said with a smile, knowing that he was trying to take Mrs Patterson's mind off the scary unknown.

A few minutes later, when Willow had just been taken off oxygen, her parents arrived, looking shocked. 'I can't believe this.

It's the first time we've left her in months,' her mum said.

'We know it's not your fault, Mum,' Willow's dad reassured the older woman. 'It would've happened if we hadn't gone out.'

Tim took them swiftly through what had happened and what they were doing. 'We need to get her to wake up so we can assess if the seizure's had any effect,' he said gently.

'Come on, darling. Wake up,' Willow's mum said, rubbing the little girl's cheek. 'Wake up.'

'Show Daddy how you clap with Grandma,' her dad added.

Willow's grandmother sang the first verse of 'If you're happy and you know it' and clapped.

Still Willow didn't wake, and Rachel exchanged a glance with Tim. The longer the baby was unresponsive, the more likely there were to be problems.

Finally, to their relief, the baby woke and started crying.

'Mum-Mum, Da-Da,' she said, stretching her arms up to her parents.

The fact that she was able to recognise

her parents was a really good sign, and relief flooded through Rachel.

Willow's mum scooped her up and held her close; the baby clutched her and whimpered.

'It's going to be all right, now,' Willow's dad said, enfolding them both in his arms.

'Now she's awake, we're going to send you to the paediatric department so they can assess Willow properly,' Rachel said. 'They might want to keep her in overnight, but if they do you can stay with her.'

'I'm never leaving her again,' Willow's mum said, her face pinched. 'Never.'

'Her gran did everything right,' Tim said gently. 'These things happen. But when Willow's been assessed they might have a better idea about whether she has epilepsy, and they can give you advice on how to handle any future fits.' He stroked the little girl's cheek and smiled at her mum. 'It's nice to see those big blue eyes. Take care.'

Once the Pattersons had gone up to Paediatrics with Willow, Tim gave Rachel a hug. 'You were thinking of your girls at that age, weren't you, and how easily something like this could've happened to them?'

She nodded. 'I'm guessing you were, too.'

'Yeah. It's a scary thing, being a parent. Everything you think you know suddenly goes out of your head, and instead there's this great fog of panic.' He gave her a wry smile. 'I'm going to be terrified every time I babysit my new grandchild.'

She smiled back. 'You might get that initial panic, but in an emergency you'll switch back to doctor mode.'

'There is that,' he conceded.

In the middle of December, Rachel and Tim were walking through Hampstead Heath. There was a mini Christmas fair going on, with a few stalls and a band on a small stage with a keyboard, a drum kit, a guitar and an amp, playing Christmassy music. When they started playing 'Last Christmas', Tim looked at Rachel. 'They're playing your song. It'd be a shame to waste it.' He gave her a bow and held out his hand. 'Dance with me?'

She laughed and stepped into his arms.

It was wonderful, Tim thought, dancing under the trees with Rachel's arms wrapped round him and her cheek resting against his, with all the fairy lights twinkling round them. All they needed now was the lightest, lightest sprinkling of snow as the final touch...

And then he heard someone say, 'Look at those two dancing together. It's lovely to see an older couple still so in love with each other.'

Love.

Was he in love with Rachel?

Her warmth and sweetness had seeped through the barriers he'd built round his heart, gently undoing all the fetters without him even noticing, because he'd been focused on enjoying the brightness she brought to his days. He was even starting to think that he could actually handle Christmas, this year—and it was all thanks to her. The world had started to feel bright and sparkling again, since the first moment he'd kissed her. Waking up in her arms in the morning made him feel that the world was full of sunshine. He was learning to see the joy again.

He almost—almost—told her. But he didn't want to say it for the first time in the middle of a crowd. Instead, he just let himself enjoy the moment, dancing with her under the fairy lights.

When the song came to an end, he smiled at her. 'Shall we take a selfie?'

She smiled back at him. 'Sure.'

He pulled his phone out of his pocket and stared at it in horror as the notifications filled the screen. Missed calls from Hannah and Jamal. Sophie, too.

And the text that stood out made his blood run cold.

Baby not moving. Going to hospital.

Oh, Christ.

No.

Hannah couldn't lose the baby. She couldn't.

And then he thought of Mandy, going to hospital in the ambulance but never making it there.

'Tim? What's wrong?'

'My phone. Must've been on silent.' He couldn't bear to voice his fears out loud. Instead, he showed her the screen.

'Oh, no. Poor Hannah. She must be worried sick. And you must be, too,' she said. 'But, Tim, remember that it doesn't always mean there's a problem. Hannah's in her last month, right? It could be that the baby's head is engaged so she won't feel so much movement, or the baby's simply in a deep sleep.

The chances are, by the time she gets to hospital, she'll be feeling movements again.'

'But what if…?' The words stuck in his throat. What if the baby died? What if Hannah died? His clever, capable daughter, so like her mother. Surely Fate wouldn't be so cruel as to repeat itself? He wouldn't lose his daughter and grandchild, the way he'd lost his wife?

He'd been so busy having fun with Rachel that he hadn't taken care of his daughter.

'Tim,' Rachel said, dragging him from his thoughts. 'We're not far from my place and it'll be quicker to walk there than call a taxi. I'll drive you. Which hospital?'

'I…' He couldn't think straight. 'Hackney.'

'OK. Call her,' she said, giving his phone back. 'Tell her you're on the way.'

Hannah's phone went straight to voicemail. So did Jamal's. And Sophie's. And Calum's.

He was shaking so much; he couldn't type a text. He called Hannah again and left a voice message. 'It's Dad. I'm on my way. Hang on. It's all going to be all right.' Even though he was terrified that it wouldn't be.

He was the parent. It was his job to reassure her. 'I'll be there as soon as I can. Love you.'

It felt as if it took hours to walk to Rachel's, even though it was only a few minutes, and his brain was too scrambled for him to talk—though at least he'd remembered which hospital. She didn't push him, simply switched the radio to a classical station and drove him to Hackney.

'Do you want me to come in with you?' she asked.

Yes. No. He didn't know. Panic and worry had rendered him completely hopeless. 'I…'

She squeezed his hand. 'Look, I'm not going to intrude. Go and see Hannah. Call me if you need *anything*. That goes for all of you. OK?'

'Thank you,' he whispered, and wrapped his arms round her.

'It's going to be all right,' she said.

Exactly the same reassurance he'd given Hannah. And he knew it was just as hollow. Mere words. Because nobody could know for certain.

'Call me when you can and let me know how she is,' she said. 'Give her my love.' Her eyes held his. 'Remember what I said.

Anything you need, I'm here. Just call me. Even if it's stupid o'clock.'

He nodded; his throat too thick with fear to let any words out.

It wasn't a rejection, Rachel reminded herself as she drove home. It was obvious that Tim's worries about Hannah and the baby had brought back memories of Mandy's death. He needed space and time. She'd done what she could to support him.

She just hoped that everything would be all right. There were several reasons why a baby's movements decreased—as well as the ones she'd given Tim, there was the chance that Hannah had overdone things that day. Plus, babies were often wide awake when the mum was trying to sleep and less active during the day.

Please, please, let everything be all right, she prayed silently. Let it be the Christmas Tim and his family needed, full of love and happiness and the joy of a new baby.

Be strong, Tim told himself as he walked up to the maternity department reception.

'My name's Tim Hughes. My daughter Hannah's been brought in because she couldn't feel the baby moving, and she needs me here,' he said. His glance flicked automatically to the whiteboard; Hannah's name was there, right under the word 'emergency'. 'Would it be possible to see her, please?'

'I'm afraid we can't allow visitors,' the receptionist said, 'but I can get a message to her and you're very welcome to go into the waiting room.'

Tim dragged in a breath. 'Sorry. As a doctor myself, I should know the protocol,' he said.

'But you're also a dad,' the receptionist said, 'and you're worried about your daughter. Actually, I think her sister's in the waiting room.'

Tim forced himself to smile. 'Thank you.'

The receptionist directed him to the waiting room, and Tim strode swiftly there. Sophie stood up as soon as he walked through the door, and he wrapped his arms round her. 'How's Hannah? How are *you*? I'm so sorry.' The words tumbled out.

She held him close. 'Everything's OK, Dad. They gave her a scan and the baby's okay. They gave her a glass of orange juice and the baby's moving again now.'

'It's the sugar in the juice. Energy,' he

said. 'Are they giving the baby a non-stress test? Did they say why the baby wasn't moving?'

'I don't know, Dad. The main thing is, she's getting checked out.'

'I should've been here.' But he'd focused on himself and his own needs instead of on his daughters. He hadn't been there when they'd needed him. 'I'm so sorry. My phone was on silent.' He dragged in a breath. 'I don't know how. I was out with Rachel.'

'Where is Rachel?' Sophie asked.

'I, um—she went home.'

'Right.' Sophie looked surprised. 'How did you get here?'

'Rachel drove me. She said it'd be quicker than waiting for a taxi.' He raked a hand through his hair. 'I said I'd call her and tell her…when I know what's happening. She… um…sends love.'

'She could've stayed,' Sophie said.

'Better not,' Tim said.

Sophie gave him a strange glance. 'Calum and I will give you a lift home when we've seen Han and know she's OK.'

'Thank you.' He hadn't even thought about getting home. 'Where is Calum?'

'Gone to get coffee. You just missed him.'

'Right.' He held her close. 'I'm sorry. I've let everyone down.'

'Han was a bit upset when you didn't call,' Sophie said. 'She even asked me to ring the hospital, because we both thought you were at work.'

It was a fair point. But he'd replaced work with Rachel. Made himself even less available.

And it had to stop.

Now.

He'd tell Rachel tonight, once he knew Hannah and the baby were both all right.

The waiting seemed to last for ever, but finally Hannah and Jamal appeared in the waiting room.

'They've checked us out thoroughly, given me a scan and done a non-stress test, and they're happy for me to go home,' Hannah said. Her voice was wobbly. 'The baby's fine. Just really deeply asleep when I couldn't feel the usual movements, they think.'

'And she'd been overdoing it,' Jamal said. 'Which means we need to tag team her and make her rest.'

'I'm fine,' Hannah said, lifting her chin. 'I just panicked a bit, that's all.'

Tim hugged her. 'I'm so glad it's all

right. And I'm so sorry I wasn't there.' He should've been there. He could've reassured her—both as her father and as a medic. 'I'll take the first shift in looking after you.'

'Dad, you've got work,' Hannah said. 'And you'll all drive me potty if you fuss. It's fine. I have all your numbers, and I'll call if I'm worried about anything. I don't need a babysitter.'

'My phone was on silent,' Tim said. 'It won't be, in future. I'll make sure it's diverted to the admin team if I'm at the hospital.'

Hannah's face crumpled, and she burst into noisy sobs.

Guilt flooded through him, and he stroked her hair, holding her close. 'It's OK, Han. It's all going to be OK.'

'I was so scared, Dad.'

'I know, baby. But it's all fine. You have Jamal. You have Soph and Calum. You have me. It's fine. They've told you what to do if you're worried in future?'

'Drink juice or have a snack. Lie on my left side and count the movements. If I'm still worried, come straight in.'

'Then it's fine,' he said. 'It's all going to be just fine.'

He went home with Hannah and Jamal and took the Tube home rather than making Sophie and Calum drive out of their way. And then he called Rachel.

Rachel snatched up her phone as soon as she saw Tim's name on the screen. 'How's Hannah?'

'Fine. They did a non-stress test and a scan, and they think the baby was deeply asleep. They've sent her home.'

'I'm so glad,' she said. 'Is there anything she needs? Anything I can do?'

'No.' He was silent for a moment. 'Rachel—I'm sorry. I can't do this any more. I can't be with you.'

It took her a moment to process what he was saying. He couldn't do this? He didn't want to be with her? 'Why? What have I done wrong?'

'It's not you—it's me,' he said.

Dread trickled down her spine. Everyone knew that phrase; it was the nice guy's get-out.

'I'm sorry. I just think it's better if we stick to being colleagues from now on,' Tim continued.

Rachel didn't understand. She thought

things had been going well between them. They were in tune with each other. They got each other's jokes. They liked each other's families. They *fitted*. She'd thought they had a future; but it seemed Tim hadn't felt the same. She was too shocked to know what to say. So much for finally moving on from the misery of her marriage and this last lonely year, because Tim had just pulled the rug out from under her. She shouldn't have trusted him with her heart so quickly.

He didn't want to see her any more.

Though she supposed that the bright side was that at least Tim hadn't cheated on her before dumping her. He'd merely made love with her and let her fall in love with him.

'I need to concentrate on my girls,' he said.

It felt like an excuse. A flimsy one, kindly meant to spare her feelings, but actually it did the reverse. It felt like a hundred paper cuts ripping across the confidence she'd built back up, each little tear bleeding into another and making her realise how fragile that confidence had been.

'Of course,' she said. She wasn't going to fall apart and let Tim realise how deeply she felt about him. She'd made enough of a fool of herself, already. 'I'll see you at work. I'm glad everything's all right with Hannah and the baby.' Then she quietly ended the call and put her phone back on the coffee table.

It was over.

All the dreams had popped into nothing, like the useless bubbles they'd really been all along—except she hadn't wanted to see that.

And she definitely wasn't feeling any of the spirit of Christmas that had bathed her for the last few days when she'd been making memories with Tim. Thankfully it was still the middle of December, so Meg and Saskia wouldn't be home for another few days. It would give her enough time to get herself back under control again and pretend that everything was fine, just as she'd pretended for the last year. But, right at that moment, the house felt unbearably empty, full of echoes, all the promise of Christmas snuffed out.

She drew her knees up and wrapped her arms round them, then rested her face on her knees and cried out all her loneliness and despair. The one good thing was that they'd kept their burgeoning relationship quiet at work, so nobody would know what a stupid mistake she'd made.

* * *

If he'd stayed with Rachel, Tim thought, he would've let his girls down again. But breaking up with her had made him feel just as guilty, because he knew he'd hurt her. Let her down, the way he'd let his girls down.

He'd done the right thing. He knew that.

So why did he feel so miserable about it?

The next few days at work were truly awkward. Rachel was fine while she could concentrate on a patient or teaching one of the students or juniors who'd been assigned to her, but when she was in her office writing up notes or doing paperwork for a training schedule, she was acutely aware of where Tim was in the department—and she just missed him.

Stupid, stupid, stupid.

He'd made it clear he didn't want to be with her.

So she'd focus on the bits of her life that did work: being a mum, being a doctor and being a friend. Anything else wasn't going to be on her agenda in future.

On the Friday afternoon, the paramedics brought in a woman in her late sixties. 'This is Mrs Dilreet Kaur,' Samir said. 'She hasn't been feeling well all week but she thought she was just coming down with a bug. Today, she'd been feeling a bit short of breath and nauseous, and then some pain in her jaw and her back—nothing in her chest, so she didn't think it was her heart.'

Women often had different symptoms from men when having a heart attack, Rachel knew, and were more likely to feel the pain in their jaw or back rather than the classic heart attack symptom of crushing pain in the chest.

'She collapsed, and her friend called us,' Samir continued. 'We've given her some aspirin, and we did an ECG in the ambulance on the way here, which shows it's a STEMI.' He handed her the printout from the ECG. 'She's on oxygen, but I'm not happy with her sats.'

'Thanks, Samir. I've already put a call up to the cardiac team,' she said. 'Has anyone called her family?'

'Her friend called her son,' Samir said, 'and he's on the way in.'

'Great. Thanks, Samir.'

Between them, they transferred Mrs Kaur from the trolley to the bed. 'Mrs Kaur, I'm Rachel Halliday, one of the doctors in the Emergency Department,' Rachel said. 'Samir put some wires on you in the ambulance so he could monitor your heart, and I'm just going to attach those wires to my monitor here so I can do the same thing,' she explained as she hooked Mrs Kaur up to the monitor.

'What's happened?' Mrs Kaur croaked.

'You've had a heart attack,' Rachel said gently. 'What's happened is that your arteries around your heart have become narrowed by a gradual build-up of fatty deposits called atheroma, and a piece of atheroma has broken off along with part of your artery wall. A blood clot formed to repair the damage, and it's blocked your artery.' A STEMI—an ST segment elevation myocardial infarction—meant there was a total blockage. 'Your heart muscle hasn't had the blood and oxygen it needs, and we need to treat you to restore the blood flow. I'm going to do some things here in the department to make you feel better, and then we're going to send you up to the cardiac unit for tests to see whether they're going to treat you with medication or surgery.'

'I'm sorry to be such a nuisance,' Mrs Kaur said.

'You're not a nuisance at all. I'm here to help,' Rachel reassured her. 'Please ask me if there's anything you're worried about. Your friend called your son, and he's on the way in.'

'What kind of surgery? Will I have to have a transplant?'

'No. It's something called an angio-plasty—using a tube called a catheter with a balloon at the end. The surgeon will put it into one of your arteries and guide it up to the bit where your artery's blocked, then inflate the balloon to open the artery again. If they can't do that, they might have to do a bypass—that's where they take a blood vessel from another part of your body and attach it to the artery above and below the blockage, so the blood's diverted—'

The rest of Rachel's words cut off as Mrs Kaur went pale, slumped and stopped breathing. The monitor showed that her heart had gone into ventricular fibrillation; it was an arrhythmia that often happened just after a heart attack, when the heart muscle hadn't had enough blood flow and became electrically unstable.

'Crash team!' Rachel yellowed. 'Nita, I'm going to need you to put a ventilation bag on her. I'll start the compressions.' She changed the angle of the bed so Mrs Kaur was lying flat, then tilted her head back and lifted her chin to open her airway. Nita, the nurse working with her, put a ventilation bag in place, and Rachel started pushing down hard on Mrs Kaur's chest to the rhythm of the Bee Gees' 'Stayin' Alive', making sure she was going down at least five centimetres. After the first thirty compressions, she paused so Nita could give two rescue breaths with the mask; the monitor showed that the heart rhythm was still VF, so she kept going for another thirty compressions. Two breaths. Still VF. She and Nita carried on, looking up when the doors to Resus burst open—and of course it would have to be Tim.

But their patient was much more important than the tension between them, right now. 'She's in VF. I'm doing chest compressions and Nita's bagging,' Rachel said. 'We're coming up to two minutes.'

'I'll attach the defib,' he said. 'OK. Charging. Let me know when you're at two minutes.'

Push, push, push.

Her wrists were hurting. 'That's two minutes of chest compressions,' Rachel said.

'And clear,' Tim said.

Everyone stood back, and he delivered the first shock.

Mrs Kaur remained motionless.

'Rachel, we'll swap for this cycle,' Tim said.

It was hospital protocol to change the person doing the chest compressions every two minutes, to avoid fatigue and make sure that the compressions were deep enough.

Rachel recharged the defib while Tim and Nita continued CPR.

'And clear,' she said, delivering the second shock.

'Still VF,' Tim said, as they swapped over. 'Nita, can you sort out the adrenalin and amiodarone for me?' He got her to repeat the dosages back to him. 'That's great. Cheers.'

After the third shock, Tim administered the two injections. One more shock, and finally Mrs Kaur's heart was beating in sinus rhythm again.

'Well done, everyone,' Tim said.

By the time Mrs Kaur was stabilised, the cardiac specialist had come down and Rachel did the handover. Back in the office, she wrote up the notes, relieved that they'd managed to get their patient back; yet, at the same time, she felt so sad. Tim hadn't even been able to meet her eyes when he'd said well done to the team.

This wasn't going to work.

But she'd only been at Muswell Hill Memorial Hospital for two months. How could she possibly walk out of the job now? She'd be letting her colleagues down. She'd just have to put up with it. And maybe at the next team meeting she could suggest taking over doing the staff rotas. Then she could make sure that she and Tim were on different shifts, so they'd have to see as little of each other as possible.

Next year, maybe she'd be able to make another fresh start, somewhere else. Another city, perhaps. And she definitely wouldn't make the same mistakes again.

CHAPTER EIGHT

'DAD, WHAT DO you mean, Christmas is off?'
Hannah asked.

'We're not going to Rachel's any more.'

'Is she all right?'

Guilt flooded through Tim. Of course his
eldest daughter's first thought would be of
an accident or something, after what had
happened to Mandy. 'It's not that. It's just
not appropriate any more.'

'Why not? I thought you were dating her?'

Tim was struggling to find the right words
to explain when Hannah sighed. 'Oh, Dad.
What went wrong?'

'Me,' he said.

'Nope. Not getting it.'

He sighed. 'You know what I'm like. I'm
a workaholic. That's why I wasn't there for
your mum. And I wasn't there for you, when

you had that scare and you needed me—I was repeating the same old mistakes.'

'You weren't at work,' Hannah pointed out. 'You were with Rachel.'

'And I wasn't concentrating on my family, the way I should be.'

'Dad, that's crazy. And everything was all right. And you came as soon as you got my message.'

'Which was later than I should've been,' he said stubbornly.

'So you're the one who ended it?'

'Yes.'

There was silence the other end, and then another sigh. 'OK, Dad. I'll let Soph know for you.'

He knew that she'd let him off the hook and it was way more than he deserved. 'Thanks, love.'

'I've got to go now,' Hannah said.

'All right. I'll call you later in the week.'

An hour later, Tim was scrubbing the kitchen clean—not that he used it much, apart from reheating things in the microwave, but the physical activity was giving him something to think about other than how miserable he was and how much he missed Rachel—when the doorbell rang.

He opened the door to find both his daughters standing on the doorstep; Sophie was holding a box of muffins.

'This is an intervention,' she said. 'Because Hannah and I can't just stand aside and watch you throw away something so good.'

Tim was too shocked to protest. The next thing he knew, he was seated at the table with a mug of coffee and a blueberry muffin in front of him.

'We knew you've been miserable all week,' Sophie said, 'but we couldn't work out what was wrong—if you were stressed about work or something—because you always close off and bury yourself in work.'

'It drives us potty,' Hannah said, 'but it's who you are, and we've learned to deal with it. Well, up to a point. But I told Soph what you told me about splitting up with Rachel.'

'Honestly, Dad. Right now it feels as if you're the teenager and we're the parents,' Sophie said. 'You're the head of a department at a busy hospital. We know you're clever and we know you save lives every day. So how can you be so utterly *hopeless*?'

He stared at her, taken aback. 'Hopeless?'

'Rachel's lovely. She's perfect for you.

Since Mum died, you've been lost and lonely and we've been at our wits' end trying to work out how we can help you,' Hannah said. 'And then Rachel came into your life, and you started to smile again. It meant we had our dad back. We were even going to have our first proper Christmas for three years.' She rubbed her bump. 'What could be my baby's first Christmas. A new start. And now you've wrecked it.'

'And neither of us can understand why. Rachel's not Mum, and she's not trying to be Mum. She's herself,' Sophie said. 'She's lovely. So tell me why you dumped her, because what Han said made no sense at all. I'm convinced it's preggy brain making her muddle her words.'

'I'm convinced it's preggy brain, too,' Hannah said, 'because what Dad said makes no sense.'

'I let your mum down. I wasn't there enough. I've put my work before my family, in the past—and I've just replaced work with Rachel. I'm making the same mistakes.'

'That,' Sophie said, 'is a really feeble excuse, Dad. Yes, you're a workaholic, but that's only part of who you are. We know it's because Granddad was frankly a rubbish parent; he always put you down when he should've been proud of you.'

Hannah gave a wry laugh. 'When I decided to do my PGCE, Granddad told me that English teachers were ten a penny and I ought to do a conversion course and be a lawyer instead, and I gave him a lecture on psychology and how rubbish he was. He sulked for *months*.'

Tim blinked. 'Oh, my God. He said something that awful to you? I had no idea.'

'It's OK. I said I hope he'd never been that rude to my mum, who was one of the wisest people I know and who did a job that was every bit as important as his, even if she didn't earn as much as he did. That I planned to follow in her footsteps and be a brilliant teacher who'd use poetry and Shakespeare to inspire kids to be the best they could be. And that, actually, money isn't the only measure of a job's value,' Hannah said. 'Then he said the nonsense about only saying it so I'd fight back to prove him wrong and get good grades.'

Tim went very still. 'He did that to me.'

'I know. I told Mum about it, and that's when she told me what he'd said to you, and that he'd always made you feel you were a disappointment to him.'

'Just so we're very clear on this,' Tim said, 'I'm hugely proud of both of you, and so was your mum. We wanted you to do what *you* wanted, not what we thought you ought to do.'

'And we appreciate that,' Sophie said.

'I'm just so sorry he...' Tim blew out a breath. 'If I'd known, I would've read him the Riot Act.'

'Way ahead of you, Dad. When he said it, I told him that putting people down all the time was the quickest way to make them feel crap about themselves rather than this "fighting back to prove him wrong" nonsense, and if he ever did it to Soph then I'd know about it and I'd scalp him. With a blunt instrument and lots of salt,' Hannah said.

Tim marvelled at his daughter's bravery at facing down her grandfather's bullying.

'When Mum told us what he'd done to you, Han went round to see him with his favourite cake to lull him into calmness. Then she told him you were a brilliant doctor who deserved much, much better from him, and she battered him with Shakespeare,' Sophie said, laughing. 'She followed it up with a poem every single day until he admitted he was in the wrong and you'd made the right career choice.' She grinned. 'You know, Han, maybe you need to do that to Dad.'

'There's no need to batter me with Shakespeare. I apologise when I'm in the wrong,' Tim said. 'I still can't get over the fact you tackled your granddad, Han.'

'He needed to be put straight,' Hannah said. 'It's not the way to treat people. Though,' she admitted, 'it's probably easier to stand up for yourself if you don't have to live with that person and feel their disapproval every second of every day.'

'You and Mum always believed in us,' Sophie said. 'You've always made us feel as if we could do anything we wanted—and we're so glad you weren't like Granddad. I think that would've turned us into workaholics, too.'

'Though you still repeat your mistakes, Dad. You're as stubborn as Granddad, in your way,' Hannah said. 'Yes, you used to fight with Mum about your ridiculous working hours. But she loved you anyway, because she understood what drove you and how you wanted to care for people. That you wanted to save people so they wouldn't miss their grandmothers as much as you did.'

'Mum wouldn't have had you any other way, Dad,' Sophie said. 'Think about it. She had a vocational job, too, and she understood how important your job was to you.'

'And Rachel will understand even more, because she does the same job as you. Her daughters will know how much she loves them, just as we know how much you love us,' Hannah said. 'But they'll also know that emergency doctors are really, really driven and they need to save people. It just goes with the territory.'

'Don't feel you're being disloyal to Mum by getting serious with Rachel,' Sophie added. 'Mum wouldn't have wanted you to be alone for the rest of your life. She would've wanted you to find someone who loved you for who you are and wouldn't want to change you. Someone who'd support you and get on with us and be part of all our lives, while acknowledging how important Mum was to us—and that's exactly what Rachel does.'

'I'm glad you were out with her instead of shutting yourself away on your own. It's about time you lightened up and got on with enjoying life. Mum would've scalped you for the way you've been since she died,' Hannah said.

'But I wasn't there when you called me,' Tim reminded her.

'Your phone was on silent. It happens,' Sophie said. 'You know what I think?'

He knew she was going to tell him anyway and steeled himself. Sophie and Hannah had inherited their mother's straightforwardness.

'It's an excuse because you're scared.' Sophie looked at him. 'Dad, I love you, and this isn't a nice thing to say, and I'm only telling you this so bluntly because being subtle doesn't work with you.' She took a deep breath. 'I think you're scared that if you get close to someone, you might lose her, the way you lost Mum. So you dumped her rather than risk losing her.'

Tim thought about it. Was Sophie right?

'Soph's right. Dad, there's always a risk. It's better to let people in than to keep them at a distance,' Hannah said gently. 'Be honest about your worries. I panic that I won't get the baby to term. Jamal's terrified that I'm going to get a pulmonary embolism after I've had the baby and die. There's always a risk with everything you do, but you have to put it in perspective. Live your best life, the way Mum did.'

It was as if his daughters had thrown a bucket of cold water over him.

And, once the shock had passed, he could see clearly again. He'd refused to let himself see it, but his girls were absolutely right.

'I've screwed up,' Tim said. 'Big time. Rachel's ex was a selfish jerk who let her down—and I'm no better.'

'Of course you're better than that,' Sophie said.

'Just call her and tell her you screwed up,' Hannah said.

'How?' Tim asked.

'If you're honest with her, tell her how you feel and why you said whatever you did, she'll understand. It sounds as if you hurt her, but you can fix that. It might take time and it'll definitely take effort—but she's worth it. *You're* worth it. Now, eat your muffin and think about it,' Sophie said.

Hannah nudged her sister. 'Are you sure you want to stay as a marketing tycoon, Soph? You'd be an awesome teacher. All the Year Ten boys would be so terrified of you that they'd actually do their homework.'

'You seriously think I want to spend my working day in a room that smells of feet, farts and way too much body spray?' Sophie teased back. 'No chance. I want all the glamour of fancy coffee and posh biscuits, courtesy of grateful clients.'

Tim tuned out his daughters for a moment.

Be honest with Rachel. Tell her why he really dumped her. Admit that he was scared of failing her or losing her and hadn't wanted to take the risk.

She'd probably find a solution, with that calm common sense of hers. But he didn't want calm common sense. He wanted her to love him, the way he was pretty sure he loved her. Though how could he ask that of her?

'Dad? Earth to Dad,' Sophie said.

'Sorry. I zoned out for a second,' he said. 'What did you say?'

'I said, I hope you're going to talk to her. Make it right,' she said. 'We're going, now. So call her. And then, when you've sorted it out, tell us.'

After he'd waved them off at the front door, he called Rachel. He was more than prepared for her to let it go through to voicemail and ignore him, but she picked up. 'Tim.'

'Rachel.' And then he went all tongue-tied. For pity's sake. He saved lives every single day. That meant communicating well with your team. Why couldn't he communicate with Rachel now?

'What do you want?' she asked, after an awkward silence.

'To see you. To talk,' he said. *To apologise*. The words stuck in his throat like sand.

'No,' she said. 'I don't think we have anything to say to each other.'

'But—'

'Sorry, Tim. You were right. It's not going to work between us. We're much better off sticking to being just colleagues.' Her voice was totally expressionless. She was freezing him out. 'I'll see you at work.'

She didn't even give him the chance to say goodbye before she ended the call.

Oh, hell.

What was he going to do?

If she wasn't even going to talk to him, how on earth could he tell her that he was sorry, and he'd made a huge, huge mistake?

Wanting to clear his head, he walked to the parade of shops round the corner and bought some flowers, then headed for the cemetery. He knelt in front of Mandy's grave, taking out the faded flowers from the previous week, wiping down all the surfaces and then replenishing the water in the vase and putting the new stems in place.

'Mand, it's all going to hell without you,' he said. 'I thought I'd found someone I could maybe be happy with. Not replace you—I could never replace you—but someone I can share my life with.' He blew out a breath. 'Except I was stupid. I got scared that I'd mess it all up or I'd lose her—not that I even admitted that to myself—and I pushed her away. I was hopeless with you, neglecting you and the girls for work, and I didn't want to make all the same mistakes over again. Especially because her ex was totally selfish. She deserves better than that. *You* deserved better.' He sighed. 'I love you, I always will, and she understood that. And I… I love her, too.'

Maybe it was his imagination, but he had the impression of warmth around him, as if he were being hugged, and he could smell the gardenia perfume he'd always associated with Mandy. And he could almost hear her voice saying, *Your heart expands to make*

*room for love. I want you to be happy. Talk
to her. Open up.*

And she was right. He needed to talk to
her; his mistake had been trying to phone
Rachel. Even a video call wasn't good
enough. This was something he needed to
do face to face, so she could look into his
eyes and see that he was completely sincere
about everything.

Though, before he tried to arrange a meeting, Tim knew he needed to work out exactly what he wanted to say.

'Sometimes it's useful when our parents are
a bit less clued up on social media,' Sophie
said. 'Rachel's friends list is open rather than
hidden. All we need to do is find her daughters and get in touch with them.'

'Meg and Saskia, Dad said they were
called,' Hannah said.

'Let me search the list. Yep, there's a Meg
and a Saskia. They have a different sur-
name—but Rachel's divorced, so that fig-
ures,' Sophie said. 'Righty. I'll send a direct
message to both of them and see which one
comes back first.'

Hello! We haven't met yet but our dad
Tim was seeing your very lovely mum. Ex-

cept he's done something stupid—he broke up with her because he thought it would be best for her.

She added an eye-roll emoji.

Which is EXTREMELY stupid of him because they're good for each other. Dad's eating himself up with guilt, and Rachel won't speak to him so he can't explain why he's made such a mess of things. Can we do a joint intervention to stop them ruining what we think would be a good thing for both of them? Cheers, Sophie and Hannah.

She showed the message to her sister. 'Anything you'd change?'

'Nope. It's perfect,' Meg said. 'Send it.'

Within half an hour, Meg had messaged Sophie back.

Your dad's lovely, too. Agreed we need to act. We'll work on Mum and get her to talk to him. Cheers, Meg and Saskia.

'So now all we have to do is hope he doesn't mess it up,' Sophie said.

Rachel's phone pinged to signal an incoming text. Meg.

Got a moment for a chat?

The years of practice she'd had in pretending that nothing was wrong would come in useful now. Even though she was miserable, she'd make sure she sounded smiley for her daughters. She texted back.

Sure.

The phone rang immediately with a group video call from her daughters.

'Is everything OK?' Rachel asked.

'No,' Saskia said. 'When were you going to tell us that Christmas—or rather Boxing Day—was cancelled?'

'How did you know? Did Tim tell you?' She frowned. But how could he have done? She hadn't given him her daughters' numbers.

'No. His daughters got in touch with us,' Meg said. 'They found us in your social media account friends' list and sent us a message.'

'Uh-huh.'

'What happened, Mum?' Saskia asked.

'He wasn't ready, and he wanted to call it a day. It's fine.' Rachel turned up the wattage on her smile in the hope of convincing her daughters that it really was fine. 'We can be civilised colleagues at work.'

'He made a mistake, breaking up with you, Mum,' Meg said. 'And he didn't do it for the reason you said, because he wasn't ready. It was because—oh, you need to talk to him about it.' She sighed. 'Mum, don't assume he's going to be like Dad. They're nothing alike. Dad never felt guilty when he'd had yet another affair.'

Rachel flinched. So much for thinking that she'd protected their girls.

'Whereas Tim's eating himself up with guilt,' Meg finished.

'Guilt about what?'

'You need to talk to him, Mum. For both your sakes,' Saskia said.

Almost on cue, her phone pinged.

'Who was that text from?' Meg asked.

'Tim.'

'What does he say?' Saskia asked.

'He wants to talk and wants to know when's a good time for him to call round.' She narrowed her eyes. 'Does this have anything to do with you?'

'Probably Hannah and Sophie,' Meg said. 'We're staging a two-part intervention. Daughters to parents.'

'We're hanging up now, Mum,' Saskia said. 'Call him. Then let us know how things go.'

Before Rachel had a chance to protest, the

screen went black. Followed immediately by a text message from Meg.

CALL HIM NOW!!!!!!

Call Tim. Talk to him. But what was there to say? He'd walked away from her—just as her ex had, and just as her father had.

Then again, if she didn't talk to him, she knew Meg and Saskia would nag until she did.

She texted him back.

I'm free now.

He texted back.

Be with you in about half an hour.

Should he take flowers? Chocolates? Wine? Tim thought as he booked a taxi.

No. None of it was enough.

What he needed to give Rachel was something more important. Total honesty.

He rehearsed the words in his head all the way from Muswell Hill to Hampstead; but the second he'd paid the taxi fare and pressed her doorbell, they all vanished. Why the hell hadn't he been sensible and written them down?

Rachel opened the door, unsmiling. 'Tim.'

'Thank you for agreeing to see me, Rachel,' he said quietly.

'Come in.' She stood aside. 'Coffee?'

'Yes, please.' Because at least then he could have something to do with his hands.

This was crazy. In his thirty-plus years as a doctor, he'd kept a cool head; he'd performed CPR countless times, dealt with horrific fractures and trauma injuries, done emergency tracheotomies to secure airways, all the while reassuring his patients and his team. Yet, at the idea of talking about emotional things, opening up to Rachel and telling her what was in his heart, he was terrified and didn't even know where to start.

He took off his shoes, hung his coat on the bentwood stand in the hallway, and followed her to the kitchen. 'Is there anything I can do to help?'

'It's fine.' She gestured to the table. 'Take a seat.'

He sat at her kitchen table, tapping the ends of his fingers against each other, while she made coffee. Maybe he should try small talk. Except he didn't know what to say.

She placed a mug in front of him and sat opposite him.

'Thank you,' he said. 'For the coffee. And for agreeing to see me.' He took a deep breath. 'I'd prepared a speech. But I should've written it down, because all the words have just vanished out of my head.' He spread his hands. 'I'm sorry. I'm truly sorry I hurt you. What I said to you... I was in panic mode. I wish I could take it all back.'

'You said,' she reminded him, 'that you couldn't be with me. "It's not you, it's me."'

He winced as she made the exaggerated quote marks with her fingers, but he knew he deserved it.

'You said you couldn't be with me any more. That you needed to concentrate on your girls.' Her face tightened. 'I've been thinking about this ever since. I think what you really meant was that I wasn't enough for you. Just as I wasn't enough for my dad, and just as I wasn't enough for Steve.'

'What? No! It absolutely wasn't that.' He stared at her, horrified. 'Is that really what you thought?'

'What other reason could there be?' she asked tightly.

'You're enough for me. Of course you're enough for me. I love you.' And then he stared at her, aghast at what he'd just blurted out.

'You love me,' she said drily. 'And that's why you dumped me.'

He raked his hand through his hair. 'I know it doesn't sound as if it makes any sense.'

'It doesn't just *sound* it. It doesn't make sense at all,' she said.

'It's all a mess,' he said. 'My job came first, most of the time, and I know I wasn't there for Mandy and the girls as much as I should've been. Worst of all, I wasn't there at the end.' He dragged in a breath. 'I know I couldn't have saved my wife. Nobody could've saved her, not with the brain injury caused when she hit her head. But I should have been right there by her side in the ambulance, holding her hand on the way to hospital and telling her I loved her when she died. I'll never be able to forgive myself for that.'

'You were saving someone's life at the time, weren't you?' she reminded him.

'A seventy-year-old woman with a heart attack. Just like my gran. The same age Gran was when she died. She even looked like Gran. I needed to be sure I'd saved her. I thought that dinner could wait, that nobody would mind me being a bit late—that Mandy would be there, the way she'd always been.' He turned the mug round in his hands. 'Work was always a bit of a bone of contention between Mandy and me. I work ridiculous hours. I always have. It started as a way of proving to myself that I was going to be a really good doctor, that I'd be there for my patients and make a proper difference.' He swallowed hard. 'Partly it was because I wanted to save other families from what we went through, losing Gran. And partly...' He shook his head. 'I told you Dad was disappointed I didn't follow him into law. Actually, he was more than disappointed. He said I'd made a huge mistake and one day I would come crawling back to him and admit he was right.'

'That,' Rachel said, 'is utter rubbish. Did he ever admit he was wrong?'

Tim gave a mirthless laugh. 'Not quite. After I made consultant, he said that my being a doctor was his idea all along and what he'd said was his way of pushing me. In his view, if he told me I was useless and I'd never be able to do it, then I'd fight back to prove him wrong and I'd excel.'

Her eyes widened. 'That sounds a bit "sorry, not sorry" to me.'

'That's what I thought, too.' He shrugged. 'I guess I can see where he was coming from—but it just made me angry all the time. I'd wanted him to support me instead of sniping. And I swore I'd never be like that to my kids, trying to push them into what I wanted them to do instead of helping them live their own dreams.' He looked away. 'I had no idea at the time, but he did exactly the same thing to Hannah. He told her teachers were ten a penny and she should do a conversion course and be a lawyer. Except she faced him down where I didn't. She's braver than I am.'

'People react in different ways,' Rachel said. 'It's what makes us human, not robots.'

'But I repeat my mistakes,' he said. 'I nearly wasn't there for Hannah when she had that scare with the baby, and my phone was on silent. She couldn't get hold of me when she needed me.' He shook his head. 'I panicked. I told myself I was letting my family down again—except this time the reason I wasn't there wasn't work, it was because I was concentrating on myself. Because I was with you. And I know how unfair that is.'

'Yes, it is,' she said. 'You're using me as an excuse.'

'I'm sorry. It's…' He swallowed hard. If he told her his fears, then maybe she'd understand and give him a chance to make things right between them. 'I haven't even been honest with myself,' he said. 'Deep down, I'm scared to take a risk again. What if I fell in love with someone and lost her, the way I lost Mandy?'

'There aren't any guarantees,' she said. 'All you can do is make the most of what you have. Because, if you shut yourself off, all you have is loneliness—and that means you've lost anyway.'

'When I met you, I realised you'd had a rough time, but you were brave about it.'

'Was I? I seem to remember telling you I didn't have a clue about how to pick myself up and start all over again.'

'But you didn't wallow, the way I have. You made things the best you could for your daughters. And you just got on with your life.' He blew out a breath. 'I'm making a mess of this, now. I'm not great with emotional stuff. I...didn't expect to feel the way I do about you, so quickly. I told myself we'd be friends, and that's honestly what I intended to happen.' He met her gaze. 'Except, the more I got to know you, the more I liked you. It felt as if all the clouds were melting away and the sun was coming back out. I was happier than I'd been in years.'

'That's how I felt, too,' she said. 'Then I realised how stupid I'd been. I'd let you close and trusted you—and then you backed off. And it was obvious I wasn't enough for you.'

'You *are* enough for me,' he said. 'You're everything I want, Rachel. You're kind and you're funny and you're clever. You make my heart feel as if it's doing somersaults when you smile. Even if I'm having a bad day at work, stuck with the suits, I think about seeing you and it makes all the clouds go away.'

This was making even less and less sense, Rachel thought. If he felt like that about her, why had he dumped her? 'So why did you back away?' she asked.

'Because I panicked,' he said. 'I know we do the same job, and you get where I'm coming from about wanting to save people, because it's the same for you. But you've already been married to someone who didn't put you first. How can I ask you to be with me, when I know I always put my job first? I can't ask you to make that kind of sacrifice.' He shook his head. 'I never meant to hurt you, Rachel. But there wasn't a choice. If I stayed with you, I'd end up hurting you by not putting you first. If I ended it between us, I'd hurt you—but not as much as if you started to rely on me and then I let you down.'

'That's pretty twisted logic,' she said. 'But the point is that *you're* the one who made the choice, Tim. You didn't discuss it with me or try to find out how I felt about the situation. Right now it feels as if you used me as an excuse for your fears, instead of giving me a say in my own future. Yes, you're right. I spent nearly a quarter of a century with a man who started off as Prince Charming and swept me off my feet, and then became completely self-centred. I would never have married Steve if I'd realised I was marrying a man like my dad, the sort who'd always put himself first and didn't bother with his kids. I wanted someone who'd love me for who I was, who'd make a family with me, who'd love my mum and love our future kids. And, yes, I made the choice to stay with him and put up with the things that made me unhappy. Maybe that was the wrong decision. But now I'm in a place where I'm comfortable making my own choices.' She took a deep breath. 'And I don't want to be with someone who uses me as an excuse not to face up to his own fears.'

'That's fair.' He looked at her. 'And I don't want to use you as an excuse. I want to face up to those fears. And I'll do it, Rachel. I won't be able to make them go away overnight, but I'll make the effort. Because I want you. I want to be with you.'

'But how do I know I'm enough for you, when I wasn't enough for Steve or my dad?' she asked. 'How do I know I can trust you?'

'You don't,' he said. 'That's fear talking. Something you need to face and make go away, just like I need to face my fear that I'll let you down. And I think that's something we can't do on our own. We need someone else's perspective to make us see things how they really are, instead of what we think they are.' He reached across the table and took her hand. 'Shall I tell you how I know you're enough for me? Because I was lucky enough to have a really good marriage. I loved Mandy, and I know she loved me— even when we drove each other crazy. She taught me that you don't have to be perfect to be worth loving.'

Rachel thought about it. Was Tim right?

Could she be enough for him? Could she let herself trust him again?

'I love you,' he said. 'It isn't the same love I felt for Mandy, because you're not her—and I don't want you to be her. I want you to be *you*, just the way you are. But I know my love's true and it's real, and it'll grow deeper with every day.' He blew out a breath. 'You know what we said weeks ago about middle-aged people being set in their ways? I'll try to be less set in my ways, but I don't think I can stop being a workaholic. It's part of who I am.'

'And I understand that,' she said, 'because I have the same job as you. Emergency medicine means you can't walk away. You need to be there and get your patient through the crisis. It's not the sort of job where you can leave a task until tomorrow. You can't even plan your day, because that's the whole point of emergencies: you never know what's going to happen or who's going to need you.'

'Actually,' he said, 'you can kind of plan your day. You don't know who your patients will be and you don't know what conditions they'll present with, but you know who's on your team and you know they're going to try their best to help people, too, and you'll get through it because you'll work together.'

'Which means,' she said, 'you're reliable. You're not going to let your team or your patients down. Just as you won't let your family down.'

'I can't guarantee I'll be home on time— or, if I'm working, that I'll even manage to get there for a family party or dinner out with friends,' he said.

'Neither can I,' she reminded him. 'If there's an emergency doctor in the family, everyone knows that and works round it. It's all about reaching a workable compromise and having a good support network. I had Mum and you had Mandy.' She paused. 'You're being too hard on yourself. Has it ever occurred to you that only a kind man who really cared would be so worried about missing things and letting people down?'

'No,' he admitted.

'Think about it,' she said. 'You told me you knew I'd be enough for you because you'd had a good marriage and Mandy taught you that nobody has to be perfect to be worth loving. I'm telling you I know you're enough for me and it's OK for you to be a workaholic, because I was married to a man who didn't care enough—and you're the complete opposite of that,' she said.

'So where do we go from here?' he asked.

She knew what she wanted, but she wasn't quite brave enough to say it first. 'What do you want, Tim?'

'The short answer: you,' he said immediately.

She shook her head. 'That's glib. I mean, *really*. What do you want?'

This was important, Tim knew. If he got it wrong now, he'd lose her. And he needed her to know that he was being completely sincere.

'I want to share my life again,' he said. 'But not with just anyone. I want someone who makes my heart beat faster when she smiles at me. Someone I really like as a person as well as loving her. Someone who enjoys the same kind of things that I do and will maybe push my boundaries a bit. Someone who'll be happy to blend her family with mine. Someone who'll encourage me to catch up with my best mate while she catches up with hers—someone who understands that you need to do things separately as well as together and give each other space to be who you are.'

Was that hope he could see in her eyes?

It made hope glow in his own heart, too. More than glow: it burst from a flicker into a steady flame.

'I want a real partnership,' he said. 'With someone who'll let me support her and take up the slack when she's rushed off her feet, and who'll be there for me when I need support. With someone who won't mind that when I'm in charge of sorting dinner it'll be a choice of takeaway or cheese and crackers. With someone who'll know that I'm not perfect, that I have all these doubts and these fears, and I'll try my hardest to overcome them—but who understands that those fears won't go away overnight, and I'm going to need prodding from time to time.'

He squeezed her hand. 'That someone is you, Rachel. But it will only work if that's what you want, too.' It was a terrifying question to ask; but she'd been brave enough to ask him. He'd make himself be brave enough to ask her. 'What do *you* want?'

She said nothing, and his stomach cramped. What if he wasn't what she wanted?

But then she cleared her throat. 'I want a

real partnership,' she said. 'With someone who'll celebrate the good times and support me through the tough times. Someone who'll do their fair share—I don't mean necessarily half of each chore, but someone who'll empty the bins or clean the windows I can't reach or notice when the laundry basket's full and put a load of washing in the machine without making a fuss about it. Someone who'll make a family with me. Someone who'll be honest and stay faithful.'

He could do all that.

'But I don't want just anyone,' she said. 'The one I want makes my heart beat faster when he smiles, just as I do to him. He's the one who makes the morning feel bright and shiny and new when I wake and see him next to me. He's the one who'll know just from looking at me when I walk in what kind of shift I've had—and whether I need a hug, or coffee made with a bit of cold water so I can drink it straight down, or to be danced round the room and reminded that life's good.'

He could do all that, too.

'I'm ready to move on,' he said. 'And I want to move on with you. I'm not offering you perfection, because perfection isn't real. But I'll give you everything I am,' he said. 'I'll respect you, I'll appreciate you, I'll compromise with you—and most of all I'll love you.' He squeezed her hand. 'I'm sorry I hurt you and I'm sorry I made such a mess of things. I love you, Rachel. Will you give me another chance?'

'Take a risk?' She squeezed his hand. 'Together.'

'Together,' he agreed.

At last, she smiled. 'Yes. Because I love you, too.'

He released her hand, pushed his chair back and walked round to her side of the table. When she stood up to meet him, he wrapped his arms round her and kissed her. 'I love you. Here's to the future.'

'The future,' she echoed.

Just then, both their mobile phones beeped with a couple of messages.

'Mine are from my daughters,' Rachel said. 'They say, "Well?"—with four question marks.'

'Snap,' Tim said. He grinned. 'Even though I'd quite like to have you to myself, this evening, I think we might need to make a video call first...'

CHAPTER NINE

'AND CHRISTMAS STARTS NOW—a day late,' Rachel said with a smile. 'The turkey's in, the pigs in blankets are cooking, the veg is all prepped, your filo pastry snake is resting in the fridge, Saskia…and I think we've earned Buck's Fizz.'

'It's so nice to see you happy,' Saskia said. 'I'm glad you and Tim talked properly and sorted it out. He's lovely.'

'He is. I think Mum would've liked him.' Rachel poured orange juice into three wine glasses at the kitchen table and topped them up with Prosecco.

'Happy Christmas, Mum.' Meg raised her glass. 'And this next year's going to be so much better.' She smiled. 'Even with exams.'

'Seconded,' Saskia said.

'Thirded,' Rachel said, not to be outdone.

'Right. Pancakes.' She'd made the batter before she'd started the veg; she cooked a pile of them swiftly on the hob, while Meg made coffee and Saskia brought out everything else.

'Do you remember when you used to use a squeezy bottle to draw pancakes in the shape of Rudolph, and give him a raspberry for a nose?' Saskia asked.

'And we'd have them with tons of golden syrup and sprinkles,' Meg added.

'And now look at us,' Rachel teased, gesturing to the table. 'Vegan pancakes with blueberry compote and dairy-free Greek yogurt.'

'Things change,' Saskia said. 'And next year will be different again. You might not even be living here, still.'

'Wherever Tim and I decide to settle,' Rachel said, 'it will always have room for both of you. And, just so you know, he said it two seconds before I could.'

'We're just glad to see you happy,' Meg said. 'And we're really looking forward to meeting his family properly today.'

'Me, too,' Saskia said. 'It'll be lovely to have a big family Christmas again.'

* * *

Just turning into your road, Dad. x

Tim scanned Hannah's text and texted back.

Locking front door now. x.

Jamal managed to park outside their gate, and Tim opened the boot of the car to stow the champagne and chocolates he'd bought as his contribution to Christmas dinner before squeezing into the back next to Sophie.

'Merry Boxing Day,' he said.

'Merry Christmas,' Hannah said. 'I'm so looking forward to meeting Rachel's daughters.' She turned her head to smile at her father. 'And we never thought we'd see you looking happy at Christmas again.'

'I'm happy,' he said gently.

'And we're glad,' Sophie said.

An hour later, everyone was sitting round Rachel's dining room table, with a glass of champagne—sparkling elderflower for Hannah, and for Jamal who was driving— and Rachel was carving the turkey. The girls had bonded immediately, and by the time they sat at the table it felt as if they'd all known each other for years instead of for a few minutes. Tim had been tasked with making Hannah sit down and stay put, and everyone else had brought in dishes of veg and trimmings, until the table was practically groaning.

Sophie had made eco crackers from recycled paper, containing a packet of wild flower seeds, a terrible joke contributed by Tim and a challenge card to do over coffee. Everyone tried Saskia's filo pastry 'snake' and pronounced it delicious; and the room was filled with conversation and laughter and the clinking of cutlery against china.

If she could preserve a moment in time, Rachel thought, it would be this one: having a full house again, feeling part of a big family, and with everyone relaxed and talking and laughing.

She met Tim's eye and was pretty sure he was thinking the same.

Even clearing up was easy; Meg sat at the piano, playing Christmas songs and making Hannah sing along while everyone else cleared the table and Rachel stacked the dishwasher.

They were in the middle of having a very rowdy game of Monopoly when Hannah excused herself from the table. 'I swear this baby's dancing on my bladder.'

She'd just walked out of the dining room when they heard a wail of distress.

'Hannah?' Rachel rushed out to the hall-way, followed closely by Tim and Jamal.

'I'm so sorry. I didn't make it to the loo in time.' Hannah grimaced. 'If you can let me have a cloth, I'll clear up.'

'Honey, it's fine,' Rachel reassured her. 'It'll take me seconds to do it.'

'Sweetheart, given that you're a week overdue, are you quite sure that was your bladder?' Tim asked.

Hannah looked horrified. 'You mean—that was my waters breaking?'

'It's a possibility,' Rachel said, 'but don't panic yet. Have you had any kind of con-tractions?'

'I've felt twinges on and off all day, but they're just Braxton-Hicks. Twinge—ow!' Her face turned pale. 'This one isn't weak!'

'Hold on to me,' Rachel said, and Han-nah clung to her arm during the contraction.

'We're going to get you to the kitchen, you're going to make yourself comfortable leaning on the back of a chair, I'll get you a glass of water, and we'll plan what we do next,' Rachel said.

'Is your hospital bag in the car?' Tim asked.

'Yes, with my pregnancy notes.' She gave them a watery smile. 'Jamal says I need to take them everywhere.'

'Yes, you do,' Jamal said. 'Oh, my God. Are you really in labour, Han?'

'It's looking that way,' Rachel said. 'It's just a matter of how fast it's progressing.'

In the kitchen doorway, Hannah had another contraction; this time, it was clearly sharp.

Rachel glanced at Tim, guessing that, like her, he'd realised how short the time was between contractions and that his daughter was actually in advanced labour.

The main thing was to make sure that the parents-to-be—and grandfather-to-be—didn't start worrying. Especially given Hannah's recent scare about the baby's movements. Which meant giving them distractions. 'Jamal, can you time the contractions for me? Tim, can you tell the others and grab Hannah's hospital bag? And, Hannah, you're doing brilliantly,' Rachel said. 'Keep breathing for me. Nice and deep.'

The next contraction came in five minutes, by which time Tim had told the others, brought in the hospital bag and followed Rachel's directions to get the thermometer, blood pressure monitor and stethoscope from the kitchen drawer where she kept the house medical supplies, and the magnetic pad and pen from the front of the fridge.

'Do you want me to examine you?' Tim asked.

Hannah shook her head. 'I love you, Dad, but—' she grimaced '—I'd rather you were at the non-business end with Jamal, talking to me.'

'Understood. And it's all going to be fine, sweetheart,' Tim said.

'Rachel, I know it's a lot to ask,' Hannah said, 'but would you? Examine me, I mean?'

'I'd be honoured,' Rachel said. 'Tim, can you take down all the stats for me?'

'For the midwifery team's records?' Tim asked. 'Ready when you are.'

Rachel took Hannah's pulse, temperature and blood pressure, and Tim noted down the readings.

'Just as well I'm in a doctor's house,' Hannah said shakily.

'You're going to be fine,' Rachel reassured her. 'Most people would have a thermometer with their medical kit, and the blood pressure monitor's a middle-aged person thing,' she said, trying to make Hannah smile. 'I'll agree that the stethoscope isn't standard, though.' She checked the baby's heart. 'All sounds good. Do you want to hear, Hannah? Jamal?'

While Tim helped Hannah with the stethoscope, Rachel felt Hannah's abdomen to check the baby's progression. This definitely felt like established labour.

'Tell me when your next contraction ends, and then I'll examine your cervix,' she said.

She was shocked to discover that Hannah was already eight centimetres dilated.

'Your hospital's in Hackney, right?' she checked.

'Yes,' Jamal confirmed. 'We were going in tomorrow for Hannah to be induced.'

'Hackney's a good three-quarters of an hour's drive from here, plus we'll need to get you up to the ward.' Rachel squeezed Hannah's hand. 'Hannah, I don't want to frighten you, but realistically I don't think you're going to make it to hospital. We'll call an ambulance, but I think there's a very good chance your baby's going to arrive before they do, because you're in active labour, and you're already eight centimetres dilated.'

'You mean—I'm going to have the baby here?' Hannah's eyes widened.

'You need to call your midwife,' Rachel said, 'and I'd like to talk to her, too. Not because I think there's anything to worry about at all, but just a quick professional chat, and you'll need to give her your permission to talk to me. Is that OK with you?'

'I...' Hannah looked dazed.

'I've delivered several babies,' Rachel reassured her, 'as well as having my own. Your dad's delivered babies, too. This might not be quite according to your birth plan, but your antenatal team probably told you that babies have a habit of ignoring birth plans.'

'Yeah,' Hannah said shakily.

'Make the call, sweetheart,' Rachel said. 'And, Jamal, can you ring the ambulance?'

Hannah called the hospital and spoke to her midwife, while Rachel swiftly read her birth plan, then handed the phone to Rachel. 'My midwife's called Naseera,' Hannah said.

'Thanks.' Rachel smiled at her. 'Hello, Naseera. My name's Rachel, I'm an emergency medicine consultant, and we're with Hannah's dad, who's head of the Emergency Department where I work,' she said. 'Hannah's doing fine, but I think we're looking at precipitous labour.' The normal length of labour for a first-time mum was around thirty hours; precipitous labour was where the baby was born within three hours of regular contractions commencing, with a sudden onset of intense contractions and little time between them. 'Is there anything Tim and I need to know about?'

'No complications during pregnancy and the baby's the normal size for dates,' Naseera said. 'Obviously you know Hannah was going to be induced tomorrow. She says you don't think there's time to get here.'

'No,' Rachel said. 'We've called the ambulance, but I think this baby's going to get here first. The good news is, Tim and I have both delivered a baby.'

'Am I on speaker phone?' Naseera asked.

'No.'

'Good, because I need to ask—given your specialty, I assume it's quite a while since you or Tim delivered a baby?'

'Yes.'

'OK. Obviously you can't list them for me, because we don't want Hannah to worry, but I'm just checking you know the potential complications of precipitous labour?' Naseera asked.

'We do,' Rachel said. With a fast labour, there was a risk that Hannah's body didn't have enough time to stretch slowly and prepare for the baby's birth and might tear. There were potential complications such as heavy bleeding, a retained placenta and even shock after giving birth, plus a greater risk of infection for the baby.

'All right. You've got the ambulance on its way, and I'm here if you need backup advice over the phone,' Naseera said.

'Thanks. We'll keep you posted,' Rachel promised, ended the call and handed the phone back to Hannah. She could see the worry etched on Tim's face and gave him a reassuring smile.

'OK, Hannah. I've had a look at your

birth plan, and I think we can tweak it,' she said. 'Just for now, keep standing, so your contractions work with gravity. I think you might be more comfortable giving birth in the living room, plus we can keep it nice and warm for the baby, so I'll get that prepped.'

'But—I can't,' Hannah said in horror. 'I'll mess up your living room.'

Rachel gave her a quick hug. 'No, you won't. Everything will clean up. The important thing now is you, and how you want to do this, and what position you want to deliver in. We'll try our best to do as many of the things you planned for the birth, but the tough thing is that I don't have anything to give you for pain relief.'

'I've got a TENS machine in my hospital bag,' Hannah said.

'We can help you put it on, but there might not be enough time for the endorphins to work, sweetheart,' Tim warned her gently.

'I can run you a warm bath, for pain relief,' Rachel said. 'Though you won't have the space to move around.

'No, I'll manage.' Hannah bit her lip. 'Though I'm scared. I thought I'd be induced tomorrow, and everything would be in hospital. This feels out of control.'

'I promise you, love, your body knows exactly what to do,' Rachel said. 'Let it guide you. And music can help your body release endorphins. Have you got a birth playlist, or is there any kind of dance music you really like?'

'I've got birth playlists on my phone,' Hannah said. 'It's a bit like my running playlist for the hard bit, and then something gentle for when the baby arrives. They said at antenatal, you match your music to your mood.'

'Perfect. We'll connect your phone to my speaker. I assume you did breathing exercises at antenatal classes?' Rachel asked.

'Yes,' Jamal confirmed.

'Can you breathe with Hannah while I get the living room ready?' Rachel asked.

Between them, Sophie, Calum, Saskia and Meg followed Rachel's directions. They put a shower curtain on the carpet to protect it and stop Hannah worrying and covered it with clean sheets; there was a stack of clean towels ready to dry the baby; and they put the heating on to make sure the room was warm enough for the newborn.

'If the doorbell goes,' Rachel said, 'that'll be the ambulance.'

'We'll go into the kitchen when Hannah's in the living room, so she's got a bit more privacy and we're not too noisy for her,' Meg said. 'Yell if you need anything. Cup of tea, hot soapy water—whatever it is, we'll be on it.'

'Thank you.' Rachel hugged her.

Between them, Jamal and Tim supported Hannah through to the living room, and Rachel brought her portable speaker through.

'We'll keep you walking about,' Rachel said, 'and we've got plenty of pillows. There's a shower curtain under those sheets, so there's nothing at all to worry about. You'll be meeting your little one very soon, and we're all here to support you. Anything you need, you tell us, and we'll sort it.'

'Can I have just the lights on the tree?' Hannah asked. 'Or will that be too hard for you?'

'I'll use the torch on my phone if I need light,' Rachel said. 'Let's make this how you need it.'

KATE HARDY

'Twinkling lights,' Hannah said. 'And music.'

Jamal connected Hannah's phone to Rachel's speaker.

'I want the upbeat one until I need to push,' Hannah said, 'and then I want the piano one.'

Jamal pressed 'play', and the beginning of The Beatles' 'Here Comes the Sun' floated into the air.

'Great choice,' Tim said. 'Are we walking or dancing?'

'Dancing,' Hannah said.

'Keep breathing in through your nose and out through your mouth,' Rachel said, 'and pant through your contractions. And we'll dance until you feel you need to do something different.'

Tim sang along, and Rachel joined him.

When a contraction hit, Jamal encouraged Hannah through the panting.

'You're doing brilliantly,' Tim said.

Four songs later, the ambulance still wasn't there—but Hannah was ready to push.

Rachel examined her. 'OK. The baby's crowning. Let's get you on your hands and knees.' And please, please, don't let this be complicated, she begged silently. Please don't let the cord be looped round the baby's neck. Please just let this work. Let this be a Christmas of joy for Tim and his family.

'I'll change the music,' Tim said, and switched the playlist. Jamal knelt beside Hannah, supporting her and telling her he loved her.

'When you feel the contraction,' Rachel said, 'push.'

Fauré's 'Sicilienne' floated into the air as the lights twinkled on the Christmas tree, and Hannah began to push.

Tim put his hand on Rachel's shoulder, letting her know he was there if she needed him. 'Good girl, Han. Keep going,' he said softly.

'That's the head delivered,' Rachel said. 'You're nearly there, Hannah. Next contraction, and your baby will be here.'

Hannah pushed again.

'That's great. The shoulders are through,' Rachel said.

And finally, the baby slid into her hands. She wiped his mouth and nose then checked him over, adding up the Apgar score. One for Appearance: normal colour with hands and feet slightly blue. Two for pulse, with it being over a hundred per minute. One for grimace, which he'd done when she wiped his mouth and nose. Two for activity, when his little legs kicked. And two for respiration, because he gave the cry she'd been waiting for. 'Apgar of eight, Tim,' she said quietly.

She dried the baby; Jamal helped Hannah to move to a sitting position, and Rachel put the baby directly on Hannah's chest so they were skin to skin, covering them both with a clean towel. 'Welcome to the world, baby,' she said softly. 'Well done, Hannah. We still need to deliver your placenta, but it's fine. There's nothing to worry about.'

'What about clamping the cord?' Hannah asked.

'No need to rush it,' Rachel said. 'The baby's getting lots of lovely stem cells and iron through the cord. We can wait for the paramedics.'

'You did it, Han,' Tim said, his voice cracked with emotion.

Jamal was sitting next to Hannah, his arm round her shoulders and his head leaning against hers, stroking their newborn son's cheek. 'He's amazing, Han. You're amazing.'

'Our baby boy,' Hannah whispered.

'Let's give them a moment,' Rachel mouthed to Tim, and they quietly moved away to the far side of the room.

'That,' Tim said, 'was such a privilege. To be there when you delivered the baby, to see his eyes open and all that wonder...'

'The perfect Christmas present. Even if he was a little late,' Rachel said.

'We were both working yesterday, so today counts as our Christmas,' Tim said. He smiled. 'And this is definitely a different Christmas, a change none of us quite expected.'

'A newborn for a new Christmas,' she said. 'A new start.'

He wrapped his arms round her. 'Our first Christmas all together as a new family—and now with our newest family member. I'll remember this for ever. We'll be talking about this when we're eighty.' He smiled. 'Today, my daughter needed me—and I was there for her. Just as you were.'

'Just as I know you'd be there for my girls, if they needed you,' Rachel said gently.

'Rachel, will you…?'

He didn't get to finish the question, because the doorbell rang to signal the arrival of the paramedics.

Once the paramedic had clamped the cord, Jamal cut it; then she checked Hannah over. 'Everything's fine. There's no need to go into hospital,' she said. 'Just speak to your midwife.'

The rest of the day was spent celebrating the baby's arrival. Hannah and Jamal hadn't brought the car seat with them to take the baby home, so Rachel persuaded them to stay overnight, and she and Tim would collect the car seat in the morning. She persuaded Sophie and Calum to stay, too.

Later that evening, when they'd made a drawer into a temporary crib for the baby, the new parents had gone to bed, and everyone else was chilling out listening to Meg play the piano, Tim took Rachel into the garden to steal a moment.

'Today's changed everything,' he said. 'I'll never dread Christmas again.'

'The day we delivered little Arun. One of the best days of my life,' Rachel agreed.

'Before the paramedics rang the doorbell, I was going to ask you something.' He smiled at her. 'Today's just underlined what I already knew. I love you and I want to spend the rest of my days with you. Will you marry me, Rachel? Make a family with me, be my love and my wife?'

'I love you, too,' she said. 'Yes.'

'That,' he said, 'is the best Christmas present of all.'

And then he kissed her.

* * * * *